CHRISTMAS TAILS
EDITED By
A PANDA

DEDICATED TO THE LOVING MEMORY OF APOLLO
You are sorely missed my friend

Table of Contents

FORWARD

Christmas is a time of Wonder. A time of Miracles! But for all the joy and light there is an equal amount of darkness. Sometimes the Light can dispel the Darkness. But not always. Life is really a Game and the Winner is the one who leaves it with the least regrets! That said both Miracles and Death abound in this volume as we touch on sorrow and joy.

Our first tail is one of desperation that becomes a Miracle. In the form of a Jolly Fat Man! This story could be a Holiday special on TV every year if you cut off the last five pages where it becomes very adult. In spite of that it is a beautiful tail. Even if it has no Dogs in it. Does have an inflatable Reindeer though. A reward for a selfless act. Needless to say it was a very Merry Christmas for this family.

Our second tail is one of Darkness and sorrow. Set on Christmas Eve it introduces you to the Hybrid Cycle. Just a taste mind you. Sort of a teaser. Though there is no sex in here it is not fit for children. A very dark tail of devastation. The Hybrid Cycle is a dark cycle and this lets you meet one of them.

Our third tail is one of true salvation. You may not think so as you read it but it is. the story of a Girl facing imminent Death and the road to her salvation. A tale of transformation beyond your wildest dreams. True there is a lot of adult material in this one. Okay Naughty bits! But it is a part of the story and necessary. Hope you understand as you read.

There is much to learn in these Tails and their pages and Morals abound if you pay attention! Even in some Immoral ways.

This is a true work of Love and i hope to see more of these characters. literally years in the making. Enjoy!

God bless the Beasts and Children!

VIXEN'S GIFT
By
PANDA MACK

Now I hadn't believed in Santa Clause since I was five, but I was totally beyond desperate so I knew I would try anything at this point. So I thought to myself that morning. "What do I have to lose?" So now I found myself sitting in the Mall watching him. He sat up there rather imposing looking on his fancy Throne all jolly all day! Finally with no one in line for the first time in three hours. Well I knew this as I had been sitting there waiting for three hours watching from one of the benches in the mall corridor. Not very comfortable! Trust me. Had a bad case of butt hurt going on by now. Santa's massive and highly ornate Throne was right in the center of the mall in front of the big fountain looking stunning there. Maybe imposing would be a better word. Like the throne of God himself! Knew to many of these children he was the bigger of the two. The glorious extravagant Christmas decorations however had been up since almost Halloween and it was now Christmas Eve so they were admittedly looking a bit bleak. The mall was closing in half hour, which is why the line was empty, and I had been here all day working up the nerve to do what I was going to do. Scared or embarrassed I can't say. Still it took a lot to build up the nerve. No where else to spend Christmas Eve!

Getting up off my bench stiffly looking around nervously to make sure no one I knew was near here I walked over and entered the fenced in area around the throne and walked through the twists of those things they use to make lines with. Hate those things but felt Santa would not approve of my sneaking under some. This however may have been worse then if there was a line. Well I was noticeable! The big guy in the red suit who had seemed very happy all day eyed me suspiciously as it was as I came through the ropes. Like he was waiting for me to sneak under one? Maybe afraid I was going to rob him? Well it may have looked like I was casing the throne. Yeah I thought of that as I went through the empty line. Tilting his head slightly as he watched me I continued to weave my way to him. The stern look on his face turned suddenly into a huge smile as I almost finished the line and he waved me forward. Encouraging me to keep it up making me smile. Had not smiled in a long time!

Patting his knee when I reached him he said in his deep booming voice, which made me think they had chosen well with him. Knew he truly looked the part as I had been watching him all day. Up close I could see his beard and hair were real. "Sit my child." When I didn't sit right away he patted his knee again and said rather seriously this time if not sadly? "Sit or leave Son. The Magic won't work unless you sit." He was Smiling again quickly. Very pleasant smile as well. A rather big Man.

Honestly? Yes I almost asked what Magic he meant but I knew he wouldn't give me an answer if I asked and it would sound rude. There was something seriously off about this guy however as he sounded like he really believed! Either a great actor or a nutcase! And he was not the usual Santa they had here for the last four weeks. Noticed that right away and as I sat watching thought that maybe the usual guy had to travel to see family so they got a last minute replacement. This guy however certainly looked the part. No fake beard or hair here like the other guy wore. Must be his own suit as well as it looked like the real thing and not that flimsy looking one the fake guy wore. It always amazed me that kids believed he was the real thing in such a cheap fake outfit. This had to be some crazy old rich guy as his suit looked fantastic up close. Thinking that mostly I was a bit big to be sitting on his lap and afraid I might hurt him I was feeling extremely embarrassed and self conscious now as he kept looking at me sadly so I sat anyway.

Oh Wow! It oddly felt very comfortable but he had muscles in those legs. Not fat legs I could tell. Smiling big he spoke in that deep voice. "Now young Man, tell Santa what you want for Christmas?" He asked and his voice was almost musical in it's deep tone. Sounded like a tone for children and kind of made me feel small. Well smaller. Already felt small on his lap. Santa is a Big Man! Not a pillow stuffed in his coat either as he pulled me close and I felt it. Santa was a really big Man! Looked so unbelievably real too. Not sure where they found him but I thought they should have hired this guy for the whole season.

Looking down at the floor in complete shame, feeling so foolish however, I spoke nervously now choosing my words carefully. "Actually Santa. I don't want anything."

His friendly smile quickly turned into a real frown. He looked rather sad now, not confused, just sad. "Then why are you here, Son?" His voice held such amazing concern and curiosity I felt compelled to answer.

"Um. It's about my Family Sir." Found it suddenly so hard to speak as the emotions welled up from deep inside me. Felt so childish and almost in tears. These words I spoke rapidly turned his frown upside down and into a smile again, so I found the courage and continued to explain to him. "Well? My Dad Sir. He got laid off from his job back on Halloween and he just hasn't been able to get a new one. My Mom? Well she's been working part time but it's not even enough to pay the bills. Their savings are gone. My little Brother and two Sisters are expecting a Christmas that is just not coming." Found myself almost in tears as I laid it out. "Now I don't expect you to get him a job but if you could bring my Brother and Sisters a little something it would help. However I don't know what they want either Sir, Vinnie is still six, Lisa is almost nineteen, and Lynn is ten. Please, Sir! If your real? Do what you can for them. That's all I ask. It hurts so much knowing the disappointment they will feel if there are no presents."

"What do you want Son? You must want something for yourself?" He asked extremely curiously sounding.

"I'm good. Help them!" Said fast getting up shaking my head and I left quickly a tear finally forming in my eye. Had thought those words for hours but saying them out loud was something completely different! Hurt so much more.

Catching the last bus home I felt like such an absolute idiot the whole way. Worse than usual. Had just asked a complete stranger for help. Some Guy hired to play a fantasy part to make the kids happy. The way my luck was going someone from school probably saw me up there like a little kid, maybe even got pictures, and I would be branded a total loser by New Year! The joke of the School for the rest of the year. Certain I had wasted the whole day. Of course Santa wasn't real! He's just a Fairytail for little kids! How stupid could I be? What had I been thinking? Oh I was horrible on myself the entire way home but when I got home and saw the sadness in my Mother's eyes as she was trying to make a rather meager supper, I knew I did the right thing as I had at least tried something. Probably a waste of my time sure, but holding up a few liquor stores was no kind of option. Didn't have a gun anyway. Sticking up a liquor store with a beat up super soaker was out of the question! Cashier would probably just shoot me anyway.

Felt like such a total failure.

Life had always been tough for us! With barely enough money in my house to pay the bills, we never had very good toys. My older sister Lisa and I were only eleven months apart in age but both in high-school still. She a Senior at nineteen and me a Junior at eighteen. We had both gotten measles at the same time and missed a year of school it was so bad. Mom and Dad still owed on some medical bills from that. Lynn was sitting happily in the living room playing with her one Monster School doll Mom found at the Toy giveaway last year, Vinnie was joyfully watching his favorite Puppy show on our small crappy TV and both seemed so happy and excited. Their ignorance shielded them from the truth. Imagining how crushed they were going to be in the morning hurt me so bad. Felt ready to puke I had myself so worked up into such a state.

Yeah I hated being poor! But what could I do about it? Turned eighteen a week ago. Tried to get a job! God how I tried! Life was so hard these days. Not just for us either I new. Then Dad finally came home from his job search seeming so tired and beaten and he just looked at my Mom and hung his head in shame and misery. My Dad was a good worker and had experience but was either over qualified or under qualified for everything he applied for. Mom just started to cry. Lisa looked up from her homework at them for a brief moment, shook her head sadly and went back to work. She was trying so hard to get a scholarship.

Going to my bedroom down in the basement I threw myself on my crappy little bed and began to cry. No longer holding in the tears and pain that threatened to break me the flood gates opened. When Mom eventually hollered down that supper was ready I yelled back quite depressed that I wasn't hungry and she should give mine to Lynn and Vinnie. It was a lie! A complete utter LIE! Oh I was so very hungry as I had not eaten all day. Not enough food in the house to satisfy my hunger. Not much food in the house. We were all losing weight as portions got smaller and smaller as prices grew higher. The hopelessness and despair were heavily crashing down on me now and I thought I would break under the immense weight. Finally I actually just cried myself to sleep hoping not to wake ever again and see their hearts broken. Could not take it anymore.

Tossing and turning fitfully not asleep but not quite awake either I started hearing noises in the wee hours of the morning when there should not have been any. Sounded like a hundred small padded feet running around. Could hear every footstep above me all the time down here. Tried to sleep more. Not successful at that either. Total FAILURE!

Giving up on sleep finally I decided to go upstairs! Hey I had to go anyway. Only five in the morning I still had not gone potty in ten hours? Maybe more. Using our small bathroom to take a quick pee first I decided to see what those noises were earlier and headed toward the living room. Quickly I could see flashes of color coming from in there and became nervous. Huh? Oh! They must have decided to put up the small artificial, oh hell cheap fake, tree after I fell asleep. Trying to make the little ones feel better probably.

Coming around the doorway into the livingroom my jaw just dropped and I froze in my tracks. Glad I used the bathroom first! There was a tree in there but the tree standing in there was definitely real and at least seven feet tall. It looked like something out of a magazine, the extravagant decorations covering it were picture perfect as well. Had Martha Stewart been here? What made my jaw drop even more than the tree though were the piles of beautifully wrapped presents beneath the tree. We are talking piles of them and I just exclaimed rather loudly. "Holy Fuck!" Could not help myself and I had kind of shouted that.

Lisa suddenly stepped up beside me, her arm rubbing on mine close, and she whispered breathlessly. "Holy fuck is right little Brother. Where the Hell did all this come from?" There was tremendous awe in her voice with the fear. "We're so broke now we're about to be homeless. I saw the Damn foreclosure notice so I know. We pay a lot now or they take the house after New Years!" This was news to me but it did not bring me down. Or would that be up? At the moment I could not tell you as I was in shock.

Mom and Dad came rushing down the stairs right then! Knew it was them as Dad was already shouting angrily. Knew he was under tremendous stress so I stayed calm! Let him get some stress out and yell. He might need it in a moment. "What the fuck is going on down here damn it? Who's hollering at this hour. Why the Hell..." They came in the living room! He spun his head and looked at Mom! She looked at him wide eyed and both of them just shook their heads in terrifyed confusion. The looks on their faces held fear but joy. Impossible to view that tree without joy in your heart. High pitched squeals of delight echoed throughout the house as Lynn and Vinnie shot past us and ran to the piles of presents looking for their names. The sheer joy on their faces was tremendous! Always wanted to see that and it made my heart swell with happiness. Was this some kind of a miracle!? Was I in a coma and this all fantasy? Seemed more likely to me. A very happy chaos ensued as Mom quickly took charge and tried to get things organized. Someone had too do it as the little ones were far to excited and might break something.

Lisa who had just stood next to me so far in shock as well, turned my way now. Looking me in the eye carefully she asked sounding extremely nervous. "You wouldn't happen to know anything about this would you? Any dead body's you need help burying?" Knew she meant that. Could see the twinkle in her eye at the joy our Brother and Sister showed. Understood then she was hurting as bad as me.

Shrugging I told her as honestly as I could. "I honestly don't know Sis! Unless you believe in Santa Clause?" Well if it wasn't any of us brought this stuff here who could it be? Only stranger I ever heard of breaking into peoples houses and leaving presents was Chris Kringle! Not sure one person could do all this in one night I suddenly remembered the sounds of small feet! Elf's? The tree and presents were fantastic. We had more than just presents though. The coffee table was covered in trays of cheese, salami, crackers, and cookies. Three Big Stockings full of goodies hung on the wall. On an end table was a sweating old fashion glass gallon jug and five amazing crystal cups. It looked like eggnog in the jug. Just looking at that big amazing bounty made my stomach growl. Lisa tsked at me and shaking her head in understanding grabbed a paper plate and quickly filled it with stunning food from the trays handing it to me. She knew full well I went hungry last night and she also knew why. "Thanks." Said it to her quite nervously taking the plate she offered and I started eating nervously while I watched Mom, Lynn, and Vinnie make piles of gifts. There were only four big piles when they were done. One for Vinnie, one for Lynn, one for Lisa, and one for Mom. No pile for either Dad or me. Odd! Kind of understood why there was none for me! Had not expected one. Well it had to be Santa! No idea how but there was no other answer now. But why none for my Dad? This struck me as oddly strange. Had not asked anything for him but had not asked for stuff for Mom!

Looking up at the ceiling however I whispered as I sat there. "Thank you Santa! Oh and you too God." Lisa was close enough she heard my words and she looked at me funny! Suddenly I was pretty sure she was going to say or ask something I did not want her too so I spit out. "Go open your gifts Sis." She eyed me a moment than smiled and went to her gift pile. She knew I had a hand in this. Dad sat in his chair with the camera which was somehow mysteriously sitting on the arm of his chair. So I sat in Mom's usual chair and watched the joy on all their faces, including Dad's, while I was stuffing mine. Hey I was hungry and the food was great! Dad knew too well how bad things were and he felt so much like a failure this moment of joy was wonderful to him.

Once all the gifts were sorted Mom finally looked at me and gave me such a very sad look. "Sorry sweety. There just doesn't seem to be anything here for you." Lisa eyed me suspiciously. Again! Did not blame her! Looked damn suspicious to me and I knew what had happened. Mom kept talking however. Trying to organize. "Okay now kids. We take turns opening them. You remember from last year? Youngest to oldest so Vinnie goes first." He didn't hesitate and grabbed the biggest one from his pile just ripping the wrapping paper from it. It was a big vehicle from his Puppy show and he squealed with such joy at it. He had said he wanted one a thousand times. This month. Oh I had looked at the price on that while wandering around in the mall in te morning. It was at least a ninety dollar toy, on sale! Both Mom and Dad seemed utterly clueless! Looked so confused. Knew neither of them got these and it made them nervous! Would you look a Miracle in the mouth?

Who else could have done this though? Was Santa actually real? Thought so very hard about that odd Santa as I stuffed my face! Try as I might however I just couldn't understand. Not without first believing! Lynn was next to open a present and she grabbed the biggest gift from her pile ripping the paper off gleefully. It too was an expensive gift! Almost a hundred and fifty dollar toy from the Monster

School collection. It was really quite impressive! More than any present I ever got. Lisa curiously lifted each of her presents carefully before choosing.

"This one is heaviest so I'll open it first!" She told us smiling. Could see her joy as well at this. Her gifts were all close in size and shape so none really stood out making her choice easy. She opened it fast and she totally freaked! So did Mom and Dad. Kind of beyond freaking myself now. It was a brand new laptop. An expensive one at that. Very name brand. Over fifteen hundred retail.

"Holy shit!" Dad exclaimed totally shocked. Thought that may be a large understatement. This was unbelievable. Three gifts and they were worth more then three months mortgage payments.

Mom looked at Dad for swearing with that look on her face. You know the look! She shook her head and said nothing about language though. Dad had already said it and tempers had been short so why take a chance. What more could she add. Three kids were impatient and had no time for an argument so all said it was Mom's turn. She tried to say no but believe me these kids can be very persuasive. She grabbed a small one and opened it. It was a coupon for a free make-over at a fancy establishment. Five hundred dollar value! She looked at Dad who only shrugged and shook his head looking so dumbfounded I felt sorry for him. Then she looked at me with such a sad look in her eyes. It hurt me for a second as I thought that she might think I had turned to a life of crime. She actually had! So I followed Dad's lead and shrugged shaking my head feigning ignorance. Inside I was kind of really scared but also so excited. How had he possibly been real? But then again I also thought. Why nothing for Dad though? That was what puzzled me the most.

They took turns opening gifts till they were all gone. Vinnie had a few hundred dollars or more worth of Puppy toys and bedding with some clothes. Lynn had an equal amount at least in Monster School toys plus a very pretty dress and other things little Girls like. Lisa had two beautiful dresses and a laptop. Stunning dresses and as she opened them she looked at me weirdly. Understood that as they looked rather sexy. She got lots of other school stuff as well but it didn't amount to much money compared to the rest. See I'd been shopping with her and Mom in the summer as I was bored out of my mind and I knew one of those dresses was about four hundred dollars. Maybe three thousand dollars worth total. Mom? Well she had the make-over, a crock-pot, some other cooking stuff and a beautiful ruby necklace. Looked very real. Therefor very expensive! Some other stuff as well.

Quickly I calculated in my head and figured there had to be close to fifteen thousand dollars worth of stuff. Rough guess too. Not counting the food!

Mom broke my reverie however when she said she wanted to try out her new electric griddle and make us a Christmas breakfast. Out in the kitchen we went and more chaos ensued of course. Well? The refrigerator was full of every fixing you could ever want for a Christmas dinner. I am talking packed in there too. Pretty sure that was Figgy Pudding in there even. We could eat for a week on this much food. Maybe two! Dad ended up making the pancakes however as Mom got excited by all the food and her and Lisa started cooking the Christmas meal we could now have. We were going to be eating well today! All week? Till next year? Oh that was next week.

Mom looked at me extremely funny in a not humorous way and said concerned and perhaps highly suspicious. "Why are you smiling hunny? You didn't get anything."

"But I got exactly what I asked Santa for Mom! All of it!" Was true! My voice was full of joy and contentment. She didn't get it. Not sure I did but they were so amazingly happy so I was. This was the greatest gift I could ever get I thought then. Mom came over to me quickly and hugged me tightly with tears running down her cheeks. Afraid it would be the last hug she gave me as I was going to prison for twenty years! Honest. She did.

Her voice trembling as she spoke. "I honestly don't know what you did or even how, but you have made this the best Christmas ever hunny. I just hope it doesn't go wrong!" She whispered in my ear glancing at the back door. Still thinking I had committed a crime and was watching for the Cops to kick the door in and haul me away.

"Everything is good Mom! Nothing will happen. No Police! No FBI!" As I said this however the phone rang. Damn right my heart skipped a beat. Nearly peed my pants. Like you wouldn't?

"Hello." Dad said cautiously as he quickly answered it looking nervously at me himself. Was early Christmas morning so it was probably bad news even it wasn't the Police calling to find me. "Speaking." He listened for a minute and the fear drained from his face to be replaced with shock. "Really?" Another pause. "Yes." Then, Mom grabbed the spatula from him and flipped the burning pancake. "YES! Thank you Sir! When do you want me to start?" Pause. "Tomorrow will be fine Sir. Yes I'll see you then Mr. Deverue." He hung the phone up and looked around in a daze exclaiming. "I just got a job!" Cheering broke out from all of us loudly. The little ones did not understand everything but they knew there was stress and it centered around Dad not working. Once it quieted down he told us more. "Not just any job either. The laborer position at the factory was filled by someone else but Mr. Deverue was impressed with my resume yet I was just overqualified, then when a new job just suddenly opened up late yesterday he thought I would be perfect for the job. I'm going to be a foreman." More cheering. "You haven't heard the best part yet. I'll be starting at twice my old salary, plus I get a company car." Everyone went wild for a moment! Yes even me. Thank you Santa, I thought so very hard as I understood why no gifts for Dad. He had come through for my Dad! Mom hugged and kissed Dad joyfully and they both looked happier than they had in years. Over his shoulder Mom gave me a strange look though. Lisa was just looking at me with utter disbelief in her eyes. Well it looked like I had a lot to do with this but how was beyond them both. Breakfast was a truly merry meal in spite of the weird undercurrent that Christmas morning. Dad had found some sausages in the over stuffed refrigerator somehow and fried them up too. We ate rather quickly though, as Mom had lots to do in the kitchen and shooed us all out except Lisa who was going to help her. Lynne and Vinnie wanted to play with their new toys something fierce. So I said I was going to my room where it was quiet to relax, contemplate and digest. Was almost ready to explode I ate so much! Well it was all wonderful.

Going down the stairs however I quickly noticed a rather strange out of place smell! Not a bad smell however. Like a mix of both cinnamon and peppermint. How odd. Got stronger as I got closer to my room and I grew nervous. Opening my door slowly I immediately spotted the beautiful and expertly wrapped gift on my neatly made bed? Did not make it myself. Was certain it was a mess this morning when I left it! Have never made my bed that nicely either. Looked like it had been made by experts. It was a rather nice sized gift sitting in the middle of it. There was an odd looking piece of paper on my blankets next to it. Like something out of a fantasy movie or cartoon. Cautiously I sat on the edge of my bed and read what was hand written in such stunningly beautiful letters.

"Dear Brett, you were such a very selfless and loving young Man. Asking for nothing for yourself! When Santa told me about that since I am the head of the Reindeer Union I was really touched by your kind gesture. It was an act of true Love, kindness and compassion! That kind of thing just can not go unrewarded. It upsets the balance of the universe. So please except this humble gift from me personally as a token of my admiration and hopeful friendship. You are such a bright kid with such potential and I hope you do well and try and better yourself. Don't ever listen to the people who try to put you down. If it were up to me they would get nothing but lumps of coal for the rest of their lives. Keep your head up and your heart true Brett. With all my love Vixen. XOXOXO PS See you next year." It was even signed with a real hoof print! Holy crap! No way could this be real! Had to be dreaming right? But was it really any weirder than the rest? Setting the paper down on my bedside table with one shaking hand while scratching my head in confusion with the other, doubting my own sanity, I pulled the box toward me.

"Whoa! Christ what's in here? Bricks? Lump of coal?" Thought all that as it was heavy. Very heavy! At least a hundred pounds! Sliding the bow off carefully, not easy with trembling hands, I set it aside. This was an unusual gift and everything about it was something special and I knew it! Afraid of it as well, true. So I wanted to save as much as I could. If this were real this was a special thing and I wanted to remember it always. Gently, trying hard not to rip the paper in the least I pulled it apart. Revealing the ornately decorated, sturdy, box inside. There was some small writing on the outside printed in very fancy letters as well.

It read: Model VX-V7, A Living Plastic Product by SNOW. A subsidy of ELF Inc.

"Well that's extremely helpful!" I thought sarcastically. Had a tendency to be sarcastic. Did not intend to be now. Told me nothing however. Just have to open it and see what the heck it is it seems. Carefully I got the paper out from under it and folded it nicely before I popped the tape opening the box. Looking in there rather nervously I saw an instruction sheet laying on top. Written in a fancy ornate script. Under it was a brown vinyl like substance folded and compressed, confusing me. A thick string was on the side laying across the top. The strong odor of Peppermint and Cinnamon wafted thickly out of this box and filled the room. The instructions on this paper were in the same fancy script as the box. Only one sheet. Quite simple. Mostly care instructions it looked like which I ignored foolishly. All I had to do was pull the cord it said at the top.

What the hell was it! A self inflating life raft. Did whoever they were think I was the daring outdoors-man type? Life raft could look cool on my wall however. What the heck? So I pulled the cord.

It all happened so fast however I fell off the bed as it burst the box when it expanded. Looking up in shock from the floor were I sat on my butt I saw the most beautiful large brown eyes ever staring back down at me. Now I assume it was life-size. Had never seen a real Reindeer so I was not sure. It was so lifelike however! Even thought I saw it breathing. Definitely beautiful. Cool, I thought, not sure what I was gonna do with an inflatable Reindeer but I really like it and it was so beautiful. Then it just spoke and I swear I nearly crapped my pants.

"Hi! I'm a Vixen model, version seven. You can call me Vixen, Brett."

IT! KNEW! MY! NAME! It Fucking talked and it knew my name. Holy Shit! Was my dream becoming a nightmare? It just started to look around my room curiously. "It's pretty cozy in here huh? It sorta reminds me of the cave were the real Vixen lives." It batted its beautiful eyes. Such long eyelashes! Tilted it's head at me as it spoke. "Are you okay Brett? Does your mouth always hang open like that? It's really kinda cute. Just like you." Oh Good Lord!

Shutting my mouth I stammered out. "Y-Y-You c-can t-talk? You're alive and talking?" Must have looked like an idiot. Totally terrifyed of course but an idiot.

It's voice was wonderfully cute and so sweet. It's tone a bit condescending however. "Yeah, um a little slow on the uptake are we?" It was just walking around on my bed as it spoke. Moving like a real animal would. Slowly it turned around checking things in my room out and I was suddenly looking at it's ass. Wow! Looked real to me. Realistic looking tooter and puffy pooter! She looked back at me and caught me staring wide eyed and open mouthed at her butt. What a nasty smile it had. "Not that slow I see. Checking out my ass and pussy already were you, you naughty Boy?" She asked sweetly and I just nodded! Well I had been and she caught me red nosed. Was definitely unable to speak. She began laughing and wiggled her rump at me! At ME! "Like what you see Brett?" Her voice was so lilting and sexy. Again I only nodded. "Want to touch it you naughty Boy? You can you know. It's your gift after all! All of me is here for you." Instead of nodding this time I reached up and stroked the side of her brown rump. It was definitely plastic but it was so warm. Like living body warm!

Yes I was scared then! Admit it freely. That there was a walking, talking, gorgeous, and sexy Reindeer made of plastic in my bed really didn't phase me. No! You see I was so afraid of blowing it here like with every other Girl I'd ever tried to talk to, I almost couldn't move. "Tsk, Tsk, here." She shifted her hips with my hand on them easily as I was petrified. My hand slid and was suddenly on her soft squishy vagina though. She pressed it back into my hand once she had it where she wanted it and she wiggled. Felt cool. Rubbing back quickly she laughed at me. "Now you get it. It is under the mistletoe so you have to kiss it." Looking I saw it hanging up there on my ceiling. Real Mistletoe! Getting to my feet with a smile I leaned into her rump and sniffed very hard. Yep! Sure smelt like butt with a hint of peppermint. Girlhood with a hint of cinnamon! Okay I'm a pervert! Admit that I've sniffed my older Sister Lisa's dirty pantys. Well I am a guy so I have three speed's, eat, sleep, and horny! Right then I wasn't hungry or tired however. Kissing her on the puffy vinyl-like vagina she giggled so sweetly and I was amazed by how soft and squishy it felt against my lips. Parts of her were rather solid and firm after all. She held still for me.

Opening my mouth I licked her there and tasted Heaven! What a sensation. The taste was so unbelievably awesome. Never had a Girlfriend so I had no idea if they tasted as good but this was great! Oh I did catch a very strong taste of cinnamon in there. Kind of amazed my tongue could go in I probed everywhere. She moaned gently as I licked firmly to taste better. Oh what a great present this was. Got a Girlfriend for Christmas! What did you get? Pushing my tongue deep into her now my nose was buried in her butt hole. Smelled like Rabbit poop and peppermint. We had a Rabbit in school when I was younger so I knew the smell. We kids had to clean the cage and I remembered that smell extremely well. It is very musty and earthy smelling if you don't know. Great! Now I wondered what the Easter Bunny smelled like up it's butt. Well if there was a Santa there must be an Easter Bunny!

Panting sweetly as I went nuts in her cinnamon hole. Snorting her aromatic peppermint poophole scent as well. "Oh Brett sweety. You go my man. Eat my pussy." And I did with such vigor and joy. My hands still on her firm hips gently caressing them. Ferociously I buried my face in her rubbery tushy and it felt quite different. Not sure how close to the real thing and honestly I didn't care. Liked this feeling one heck of a lot! Finding her swollen Reindeer Girl Nub I redoubled my efforts on it and she whimpered and moaned. Hey I may have been a virgin but I had surfed enough sites and read enough to know what I was doing. Having knowledge is not the same as having experience though and I prayed I was doing good. From the sounds she was making however I figured I was. So badly I wanted to please this walking talking plastic beauty completely. Yes she was adorably cute. Just take my word on that. The hardness in my pants was the only proof I needed of her adorability. Sure she said she was mine but for me it was all about her!

Pulling back I asked. "May I fuck you my gorgeous Vixen?"

What a naughty smile for a living plastic Reindeer! "By all means Brett hunny, please show a Girl what you can do." She squatted down on her belly on the bed and I undid my pants very happy. Well I asked and she said yes. Pretty sure it was not a dream anymore I looked forward to this. Well I knew she was exceedingly moist and my Manhood slid in her Reindeer Womanhood so smoothly. Was in ecstasy myself! Holding her hips firmly I began thrusting my shaft in and out. Her voice so adorable. "Oh you are big! Take me Brett, I'm yours Handsome." She even panted naughty like, like the Girls in those movies.

"That's it, take it for me baby. I want you so bad Vixen." Well I was going good and hard and she stopped talking and just began moaning while I grunted. "You are so sexy and gorgeous Vixen! Sorry but I need to loose my seed inside you. Is that okay?"

She nodded hard and gasped. Able to feel her second orgasm as she pulsed on my cock, I exploded. My legs were no longer able to hold me up and I collapsed across her back. There was a definite hard structure inside her it felt. Gently I told her. "You are absolutely amazing gorgeous. I wish you had been here sooner."

"The Magic can only happen at Christmas Brett. I could never have come alive unless you opened me on Christmas morning." Must have looked disappointed. "Don't you worry though! Now that I am alive I am good for one year. If you're nice enough maybe Santa will bring you new batteries for me next year." She turned her head back toward me. Her eyebrows went up suddenly. "OH hi! I'm Vixen!"

Sliding off and to the floor I turned and saw my big Sister Lisa standing in my doorway. "Oh shit! I can explain Sis! Well I can't explain. God I am so embarrassed. How long have you been standing there?" She was standing in the door to my room. Staring? Grinning?

"More then long enough dear Brother. That! Is some present." She started looking around and saw the ribbon and wrapping paper. Then she spotted the instructions on the floor. She just walked in and closed the door behind her like it was her room! Nothing odd there. Privacy around this house was a Sin! Picking up the instructions she sat on MY bed beside Vixen and began to read totally ignoring my semi-nakedness. Well I hope! Did not look up so she may have been checking things out. Reaching out she began stroking Vixen's back as she read. Petting her.

"Psst, Brett! Pull your pants up." Vixen said quietly and I turned beet red. How embarrassing was that? Forgetting to pull my pants up with my Sister here. Quickly I pulled them up. "He turns such a pretty shade of red doesn't he?"

My Sister laughed. She had been watching! Her voice conspiratorial. "Why do you think he lives down here in the basement. Mom caught him masturbating upstairs!"

"Fascinating! Please tell me more?" Vixen said softly.

"NO!" Now I shouted. Holy Crap this was getting dangerous.

Vixens tummy grumbled. "All this sex has made me hungry dear."

Turning toward her in astonishment I asked. "You eat?"

"Yeah, mostly carrots and candy-canes! Maybe some hay. Didn't you read the instructions before you pulled the cord?" Vixen asked sounding shocked.

Lisa answered her with humor in her voice. "He never reads the instructions, Vixen. Yes brother she eats, she sleeps, and she pisses and shits. She is alive to all extents and purposes it says. And I am not cleaning up after her for you."

Apologizing profusely like the idiot I am sometimes I told them both. "I am so sorry Girls. Now I will read these instructions." We sat there like that for a few moments in silence before I asked curious. "Why did you come down here Lisa?"

"Mom was totally worried about you. You were acting so weird! She didn't want you doing anything stupid after all. You should just be glad I offered to come check on you. Mom would have had a heart attack!" Crap! I was almost caught by Mom! Again! "We do have an awful lot of carrots in the fridge. I'll go get some." Handing me the instruction sheet I quickly began reading. Lisa got up and left only to come back a few minutes later with a big bunch of carrots. She fed Vixen while I read sitting on the floor using Vixens sweet gorgeous ass as a pillow. Didn't even mind when she farted on me. Yes I had read the part about bodily functions and she had them all. It was such an earthy scent mixed with peppermint just like her cute butt-hole.

"You know? I think you and I could be good friends Lisa." Vixen said looking up at Lisa with those big eyes. "We can double team Brett!"

Lisa replied. "I'd like that Vixen. As long as I don't have to see his pasty white butt that often. It's blindingly bright you see?" They both laughed at my expense. Story of my life! Normally when Lisa did this I got mad but let us face it! Things had changed! Lisa and I eventually got up to go upstairs. She wanted to check out her new computer and so did I. "Hey, aren't you going to kiss your girlfriend bye?" Lisa asked sternly before we left.

"Oops! Sorry Vixen. Never had a Girlfriend before." Slowly I leaned in and kissed her gorgeous lips. Her rubbery tongue went in my mouth fast and it was like an electric shock. "I'll be down in a while. Can I get you anything?"

"Something to drink. But right now I think I need a nap. See ya later, sexy. Are you coming back Lisa?"

"After supper I will. I'll bring my computer down." We went upstairs.

Mom saw the smile on my face and got nervous. "Brett are you okay? You didn't get anything but you keep smiling?"

"Mom! Just seeing the looks on everyone's faces was the best thing ever." Was honest! It was all I wanted.

"He has a new girlfriend too." Lisa piped in. "A real cutey."

Shrugging I asked trying to change the subject before things went bad. "Hey can I do anything to help?"

It worked as it got her off track. "No hunny we have most everything going. Why don't you go watch your Brother and Sister so they don't fill up on sweets. Those stockings were packed/"

"OK Mom." So I did. Lisa took some water to Vixen while I played with them both. Their toys were so cool and they loved them. Of course I ate a ton of snacks. We had the best Christmas supper ever that day and I said as much. Mom wanted to thank God and I said quickly. "Don't forget to thank Santa Claus!" All through dinner I was wishing I was eating Vixen again, so I was smiling. Well I knew what I was having for midnight snack!

Still gonna be a good Boy! Santa sees all. Can't wait till Easter!

A COLD NIGHT IN HELL
By
A NONNY LLAMA

"Wow that snow is coming down hard already. Hope your Mother can make it home guys." My Dad said rather nervously looking out the front door. We could hear the wind inside the house. The News Lady said it was a big storm.

My older Sister Ann, eleven already, was snotty as usual from where she sat on the floor watching TV saying. "She better make it home! If we have to wait to open presents in the morning, I'm gonna be mad!" She was greedy as well. Rather practical as well. She didn't see the beauty in the world around her as she never took the time to look. To busy talking!

My little Baby Brother was in his room asleep in his crib already. Dad had just put him in there before looking out the door. Me? I was sitting on the couch in my blanket all comfy. The huge Black Dog we had named Grendel had his huge head on my lap. So warm. He showed up back at Thanksgiving. He was a mix of some kind but quite large. He had been hurt bad when he showed up on our doorstep. Both Mom and Dad were big softy's and we gradually nursed him back to health. Took a liking to each other right away him and me. Such a big fluffy and friendly thing he was. Pure Black too. Like Obsidian! He stayed by me always now. Mom said it was cause I feed him but I was not to sure. Would even follow me into the bathroom and lay at my feet while I went. Kind of weird the way he stuck so close but I liked it. Dad said he was protecting me, Well, I had been the one to feed him as he healed so I figured it was just Bonding like Dad said. Dogs like to Bond I knew. Still it seemed odd. His behavior was not much like a Dogs.

Was Christmas Eve when the darkness came and took people away and we were waiting for Mom to get home from work to eat. Totally ignorant of what was coming for us very soon. There was death out in the night. Even I was excited for Christmas this year. The Weather Lady had said the storm was a doozy, what ever that is. Coming straight down from Canada! Canadian's were attacking us with it uncle would say! Canadian's are Evil! Uncle Says. Just hoovering up above us waiting to strike! Mom says Uncle is nuts! Was inclined to believe her. As he is her Brother she should know this. Could hear the wind howling over the TV it was so loud and strong. Said on the news it was gonna be a White Christmas! No Duh! They are really silly on the News so much. Keep telling us the same thing over and over like we're Dumb or something. Always liked the snow however. Sure it's cold but it's fun to play in. Mom usually calls it bad words.

Grendel's ears came up suddenly on my lap but otherwize you could not be sure he was alive. Huge Black lump on the couch. Took up most of it which is why my Sister Ann was on the floor. Just one more thing to thank him for. His fur was pure Black, unnaturally so Grandpa said, and rather thick, okay fluffy, yet so soft and I loved it.

Dad was pacing rather nervously now, he does that a lot, and Ann was just eyeing gifts under the tree like she was a criminal and gonna steal them. Was almost dark outside as I got dark early now and the tree was lit up all pretty. Some house lights were on as well but not a lot so the tree looked cooler. Felt myself getting tense for some reason however when I felt a rumble deep in Grendel's chest vibrating my legs and the couch, not a growl however. Felt my tension grow fast. Like when I was little and about to lose it! Usually because my Sister would tease me so mean. Was sure she hated me. They interrupted Cartoons to say the temperatures were falling fast earlier and she threw a fit. Big deal! We were warm in the house. Had lots of fuel in the big tank outside as well. Loved to watch the truck when they delivered fuel. It was so cool. They were here just three days ago so the tank was full. We lived a ways out from the city on an old farm in a small house. Still had the small Barn out back but we had no animals. Just Chickens and they ain't animals. Their Birds! Well except the Cat until Grendel arrived. The Cat liked my Sister! Grendel was so well behaved that Mom and Dad assumed he was lost and had tried to find his owner but no one came. They were sure the part of his ear that was missing had contained a micro chip. He was a really big Dog and Mom had been worried about that at first, mostly because of the Baby, but he was so gentle. Especially with my Baby Brother. Oliver was one and a half. My big Sister Ann was eleven and I was nine still! Grendel was not very old either Dad said. Only two or three. Mom and Dad were both really old! Thirty one and thirty two! Grandma and Grandpa up the hill were older than Dirt! Well that was what Uncle always said. Mom tells me not to listen to Uncle as he is full of Hooey! What ever that is? As he is her Brother however so she should know. I think he is funny.

Was completely Dark outside before things went bad. The world seemed so normal really. Dad was nervous, as usual, but Ann and I were happy it was Christmas. Rather festive in the house actually. Knew Grendel was awake as his snoring had stopped a while ago. Was enjoying the vibrations of his snores on my legs. Found petting him was always comforting to me so I still was as Dad's pacing was getting annoying! Every time he opened the inner door or the curtain we could see how deep the snow was getting. Gonna be deep in the morning. Grandpa was gonna have to plow us out. Again!

Once again Dad opened the inner door and Grendel's eye opened this time. Like maybe he heard something? He began sniffing hard as well and I tried to remember if I just farted. Within moments however he was up and moving toward the open door. A low growl growing in his throat. Dad and I both looked at him oddly. He had never growled before! Such a deep and powerful sound now came from him. He drew close to the door and suddenly turned. Without hesitation he went in the kitchen instead. Straight too the door to the back room. You could go outside from there or down to the basement. He sniffed hard at the crack at the bottom of the door and his growl grew deeper. Much deeper and menacing. The hair on the back of his neck bristled. Could see it and it made me nervous as it looked scary.

Disturbed and startled I went to him still. Concerned. Asking him very scared sounding. "What is it Grendel? What do you smell?" Knew he was a remarkable Dog. Dad told me stories about stuff Dogs had done and I felt Grendel could do more. Finding people buried under rubble! Finding their way home over a thousand miles away.

Dad was growing nervous as well but for very different reasons. I was thinking Grendel was scared but Dad could see by his posture Grendel was ready to attack something and he feared, foolishly, it would be me. "Mikey! Stay back!" Dad said grimly. Ann was getting upset now by all this as we were interrupting her cartoons and went to say something when Dad hissed sharply. "Quiet Ann!" He ran to his bedroom fast and grabbed his gun. Knew where he was going as he went. We had watched "Old Yeller" earlier. Not sure why they showed something that sad at Christmas. By the time he came back out with his rifle I had moved back by Ann. Trying to keep her safe and reassure her. Dad raised it to his shoulder and pointed the Gun at Grendel commanding firmly. "Grendel! Lay down!" Grendel was very well trained we thought and knew all the commands. Why Mom and Dad assumed he was lost. Every time some one on the TV spoke German he would whimper. See? I noticed these things. Well about him.

The Dog looked back at Dad and I swear it shook it's head sadly. Like it was ready to cry? Turned back to the door fast and slammed his head into it hard. Like he wanted through it. Heard the wood cracking he hit so hard. Slammed it again and Ann screamed. "Oh God! He's Rabid!" Finally! Now she caught on to what Dad was thinking. This was not the actions of a Rabid animal however. These actions were very deliberate I felt. Heard Dad cock the rifle. Knew in my heart he was about to shoot my Dog and went to get in front of him! He was about to yell at me when we heard the sound of breaking glass in my little Brother's room! Grendel spun, actually swearing under his breath, I heard it, and headed that way like Black Lightning! Grendel Spoke!

Moved far to fast for Dad to shoot so we followed fast hearing savage sounds. We got there in time to see Grendel grab a second large ugly Rat like creature by the spine from the crib in his teeth and he shook his head so very, very hard and fast we heard the creatures spine snap. A sickening sound to be honest. Grendel flung it next to the first dead body. Another was coming in the broken window already, looking so disgusting and misshapen. Dad raised his gun and fired fast. It vanished from the window as the bullet hit it. Dad could shoot. Looked at the dead ones. They were things from the worst nightmares!

Ann screamed as Grendel lunged for little Oliver in his crib. Dad swung the gun down toward the Dog and I stepped in front of it! Again! Knew the Dog was not a danger to us! Delayed Dad long enough that Grendel grabbed the Baby by the onesie and leapt out of the crib! With the Baby. Several more mutant Rats were coming in the window distracting Dad! Much bigger than a regular Rat I knew, they had one at school last year, maybe the size of a fat house Cat, with mangy looking grayish black fur and glistening red eyes. There were flecks of blood on their lips and I knew our Chickens were dead! Poor Chickens!

Rapidly we followed Grendel from the room and Dad shut the door fast and hard. Locking it! Not a strong lock or door but it was at least something. Ann was crying as Dad got the Baby from Grendel who released Oliver easily to him. Dad checked the Baby quick for any injury but I knew Grendel would never hurt the Baby and he had kept Them from Oliver. Had bonded with the Dog well and understood him. Well at least enough. He used to follow me every where but now he was acting very much like he was in charge all of a sudden. He seemed to know these creatures however so I looked at him nervously.

Kind of why as everyone else was panicking I turned to the great Beast and asked him calmly like I expected him to answer. "What were those things?" He was a Dog! Right?

No one except the Dog paid attention to my question but we all heard his reply. "Waste product from Hell! Someone turn up the heat all the way now! They'll take out the power and then it's Gonna get cold in here soon!" See? The Dog said that like he was in charge! As they all stared at Grendel with their mouths open we heard a loud crash in the basement. Grendel snarled. "Stay together! Bundle up as warm as possible! We need to leave now!" And he headed for the back room door all bristly like Genghis Khan entering China! I think! Very impressive still.

Dad and Ann just stared at him but I understood and grabbed coats. Dad spoke gravely. "We can't walk anywhere in this!"

Grendel never turned but he spoke so coldly. "Then stay and die. These things will kill everything remorselessly. That German Bastard was proud of them when he found they existed! His ultimate killing tool." Then the lights went out and Ann screamed! Shoved her coat at her and slipped mine on going for boots fast. Was not pitch dark in here as the snow gave off some light and the nightlights had battery backups just in case. Dad took his coat from me and bundled the Baby in it fast. We stood and listened to the howling wind outside. Grandma's house was about a half mile away but the storm outside was bad.

The loud noises coming from the basement were not loud enough to drown out the sound of a car pulling in the driveway however. Ann cheered up at the sound shouting as she ran to the front door. "Yes! Mom's home!" Like Mom could save us? Just snap her finger and make the Monsters disappear! Have I told you my Sister was delusional?

Grendel snarled. "Wait! Don't open that door!"

Ann opened the door and all we saw was Mom getting out of the car looking at the house. Dad swore just as I spotted the black shadows with glowing red eyes all over in the snow behind her! Hundreds of them! The headlights stayed on for a minute or two after the car was shut off so we saw far two well as Black Death swarmed our Mother before she got ten steps! Ann shoved the storm door open before we could stop her and ran out screaming for her Mother! Dad tried to grab her but his arms were full of gun and Baby and he missed. Shoving the Baby in my arms he raised his gun and fired! Hellspawn died with every shot. The rifle only held seven shots and he used them all for nothing! Did not make a dent in their numbers and they tore my Sister apart as well turning the snow red!

Watched in horror holding my Baby Brother as my Sister and Mother were completely torn apart by evil in the snow! Quickly the white snow was red all around where they had stood! My last image of them ever as Dad slammed the big inner door shut in tears, ending the sight!

Grendel snarled out grimly with authority. "If you have more ammunition human I suggest you get it. Won't save us but may buy us a few seconds. Could be all we need."

Dad asked in shock staring at the massive brute. "What are you?"

Grendel snickered wickedly at that still alert. "Illegal genetic experiment. A very evil Man made us. These things are failures he cast off to die but they thrived. Stupid Doctor did not realize. Nature will always find a way. That is what cost him his life! Thinking he could control nature and bend it to his will! We thought these things were destroyed with the Doctor when the Compound was destroyed. They breed like real Rats however so if one pregnant female survived they would. Now move human or we all die! We have to go!" Dad ran for his bedroom and the ammunition. He was not going to argue with a talking Dog. Not while death was swarming outside. We had underestimated them however!

Several things happened at once while Dad looked for his ammunition, and none of them were good. The window in Dad's bedroom shattered and a couple furnace vents popped open where I was in the livingroom, spewing forth Black Death. Explained all the noise from the basement. They had gotten into the duct work! Grendel spun and came to my aide as they swarmed me and my Brother. Several intercepted him from side just before he reached us however. His mighty jaws killed Death but they were totally Legion! They were pouring from the furnace vents by the dozen. Heard Dad fighting for his life in his room as little Oliver was pulled from my arms by a pair of them. Felt one bite my leg painfully dragging me back as I kicked out trying to save my Brother. Watched as another sunk it's teeth into Oliver's face. Heard someone screaming in a high pitched voice. It was me screaming as I kicked at them where they were tearing at my clothes. A dozen of these things were swarming on Grendel! Watched in horror as my Baby Brother died as I fought off three of them attacking me in tears. They had to be about twenty pounds apiece and utterly bloodthirsty! Got bitten several times before Grendel could finally reach me.

Just as one found an opening and prepared to sink it's teeth in my neck I heard Dad's gun roar and it just vanished it flew away so fast when the bullet slammed into it. Dad was in tears. Bleeding from a hundred places as well. Grendel was bleeding too but nothing fatal. Dead Monster bodys lay scattered around him. He looked at the remains of the Baby and this now savage killing Monster of a Dog wept. Oliver's torn lifeless body was scattered about, unrecognizable, as well.

Sobbing back tears Dad asked and I heard the pain in his voice. Saw he was in bad shape. He was covered in his own blood. "Grendel? Can you get Mikey away from here safely?"

Grendel turned to Dad and raised an eyebrow. "Yes I can carry him. But not you as well." The great Brute said this sadly. Dad was not standing up. Crawling to the kitchen we watched him. A huge gash on his leg showed the bloody muscle underneath. No idea how he got that but it looked bad.

Dad smiled at the Dog. "That's okay. I'm staying."

The Big Black Dog looked at him curious now. Cocked it's head and asked. "What are you planning on doing human?"

Dad pulled himself up on the stove and blew out the pilot light and spoke through gritted teeth. "Going to Hell! Gonna take as many of them with me as I can however!" He turned on the propane gas with a hiss.

Grendel said with reverence lowering his head. "You are one of the good ones Human. I thank you." The mighty brute raised his head and howled! An eerie sound to say the least. So deep and resonating the windows rattled. Then his voice cold and serious. "They will come now. All of them! Be ready human. Good luck. Mikey climb on my back quick and hang on! Do not choke me." They were coming! Could hear that all to well. Trying to tear their way into the house from the sounds of it. Grendel's howl called them somehow. They seemed in a frenzy.

Dad choked back a sob saying. "Love you Son!"

Said I loved him back but I don't know if he heard as Grendel moved like the raging wind outside. Straight through a broken window into the deep howling snow. The powerful winds bit into my exposed skin fast but I held on. Told the dead I loved them as well through my tears, as Grendel tore through the powdery snow with me on his back.

He panted out as we got close to Grandma's house. "I'll leave you on the doorstep. Just go in. I can not stay any more my young friend. They can not find me. I will not let them take me."

Somehow I understood. He was going to leave me and I would have no one. "Please don't leave me too?! I Love you!" He seemed thoughtful for a second so I added. "I will never tell anyone about you Grendel! I will keep you safe for a change."

The night behind us suddenly became as bright as a sunny day a second before the roar of the sound shook the world and my Father died! Began to truly cry now myself. So very hard. My family was dead! All gone! Grendel slid me off his back onto Grandma's doorstep and walked away as lights came on outside. Shaking his head he turned back and lay on me. Licking the blood from me whispering. "Love you too kid."

Grandpa opened the door and gasped as he saw us. Grendel looked up and whimpered. The flames from the house cast an eerie reddish glow on the snow even this far away. Grandpa scooped me up and took me in to safety. Grandma ushered Grendel in as well and he came to me. Just held him and cried when they set me down! He was all I had left!

Grandma said terrifyed. "I called 911 already. Is Mikey okay?" She glanced at Grendel. "Did that Dog do this?"

Grandpa was kneeling next to us looking at my wounds. He looked up at Grandma and said grimly. "No Laura. No Dog did this. Get me the first aid kit!" Let him get my clothes off and went right back to Grendel, clinging to him.

Grandma asked me. "Is anyone else hurt?" Grendel looked up at her then down at me before he spoke.

"All Dead!"

BITCH
Or
A CANINE CHRISTMAS
BY

PANDABUTT

CHAPTER 1 JOB OR DEATH Wednesday December 19th

My name Was Mallory, and I was so far beyond desperate while I was her it was almost funny! Mostly sad and pathetic though. Needed to escape from where I was and get away right now before someone ended up dead! Namely ME! Never understood how I got myself in these situations but looking back I see I was good at finding them. He, my current abuser, was an abusive asshole from the start of our relationship and at the end of his sanity now I feared! His behavior had been growing more abusive and erratic the last few weeks. Certain he would kill me soon if not right now when he found me I was looking for salvation. He would find me however as I had no where else to go. My family home was worse than a dead end. Came from a piss hole little place where people would spit on me sometimes. Most of the citizens totally hated me there! Don't worry. I'll get to that stuff before long. Very depressing and not important yet so it has too wait. College had just been a means for me to escape that horrible place and I struggled so very hard to get there! Then as soon as I got to the College like a suicidal idiot I let some sweet talking sadist charm the pants off me! Literally. Well I was desperate for affection. Had been my entire life but never found any. Ending up in a worse Hell than the one I left. At one time Home had been so much worse but for the last few years it was only miserable there.

Getting up to leave the quaint off campus cafe, filled with despair, hoping my death would be quick at least, that I was sitting in for the last hour trying to think, mostly wondering if it would hurt to freeze to death, I spotted the bright pink 3×5 card on the jobs bulletin board. (Wow! Some sentence huh?) Cafe was just off campus and students came here often so lots of jobs got listed there. Some were actually permanent positions but most just temporary. All it said in large bold print on this card was simply. "Needed! House and Dog-Sitter for holiday break." And a local number to call. No name! No nothing else! Writing was rather neat but not too neat and seemed like a sane and to the point actual person wrote it. You should see some of them on that board! Look like they were written by preschool drug fiends Jonesin for a hit! Honest! Had seen a few written in crayon. There was one right next to it looking for a Holiday Butt Slave! Okay it sounded interesting but would not keep me alive! Yes I read it! Kind of liked it up my butt. Today of course had been the last day of class till next year though so I assumed the House-Sitting job was already filled and they had just not gotten around to taking the card off the board yet but like I say I was totally desperate for anywhere to stay but here. So the Cafe would only be okay for the moment I had thought but came here as he was not allowed any more! But I knew they would kick me out sooner or later. You read that right up there! Yes I was not suicidal, at least consciously, but I knew my days were numbered without a big miracle and had accepted that! Like the stages of a medical death sentence I had achieved acceptance! Weeks at best before I was dead no matter what I did. Perhaps only days, maybe even just hours if I didn't find a safe place to stay for a while! Knew He was extremely pissed at me so he would probably kill me when he saw me! Yes it would still only be a temporary fix to go House-Sit I knew but at least I would have time to think! Needed some time to think. So this possibility actually intrigued me. The clerks kept looking at me and whispering amongst themselves since I came in. Guess I was a sight. My lip was really split and swollen bad I knew, one eye was dark black and swollen, ribs hurt bad from where he hit me repeatedly last night like the punching bag he said I was because I did not want to go to a stupid party with him because I had cramps starting. Bounced my head off a door frame a few times and called me an ugly waste of space and a piece of shit before he left me laying on the floor bleeding last night. Could have been dying and he still would not have cared. Might even be a cracked rib in there as it hurt so much to just breath. Had finally fallen asleep on the couch after managing to crawl to it, crying myself hard to sleep just after he left. When I woke up this morning in lots of pain, and a sane moment of panic I had just run out of the apartment still in my same blood stained clothes. Pretty sure there was a Girl in our bed with him as I saw a sweater on the hall floor that was not mine and bright pink, suspected who's it was, so I had not gone in to grab clean clothes or I would know for a fact who it was. If it was who I suspected and they woke up I would be dead! Well I know her Boyfriend and she could not take a chance I would tell him. Just grabbed my Bookbag, purse and beat up coat and went to class looking like I had been run over by a truck. No one there even said shit about the way I looked all day. Got some stares from most but not a word of sympathy from any of them. Made me feel even more like a piece of shit! So callus and shallow the self righteous pricks! How I hated people.

 Nothing to lose except my life it seemed so pulling out my crappy cellphone I took the card down. Hopeful I called the number on the card just praying for a miracle with all I had. A Man answered in a sophisticated and mature yet pleasant sounding deep voice rather quickly it seemed! Like he had been waiting for my call? "Hello? How may I help you?" He asked.

 When I told him fast, probably sounding desperate, that I had called about the posted job at the cafe and hoped it was still available, I just knew I sounded desperate and expected him to hang up, he sounded so relieved though. Like I was actually his salvation! Thought maybe he was just one of those types you know? Everything in his life was a catastrophe! If I had known I actually was his salvation I may have hung up! Asked me right away if we could meet now sounding rather excited, or was that desperate, so I told him who and where I was. He'd be there shortly he said and please not to leave here. Said I would wait and he thanked me again. So I sat back down and had another cappuccino with most of my remaining cash and praying to any God who could hear me that I wanted to live, I watched the door finally hopeful. Knowing in my heart he was only a Drama Llama. You know the type? Everything was a disaster! Everything life or death! Was not wrong on that Life and Death part at least unfortunately.

Did not think this could be him when he came in through the front door as this Man did not fit my expectations! Very handsome really and not too old after all as the voice had sounded quite mature so I sat and did not react to his presence. Well, I mean I had seen this Man often on campus before. He was a Teacher of some sort at the college I assumed and was not expecting someone from the school! No idea what he taught. Okay I assumed all this as he was always going over papers every time I saw him around campus. Very intently too. Could be administrative I guessed. Never seemed dangerous. Handsome in a nice way. Kinda short wavy black hair. Not quite movie star good looks but he would make a good supporting actor. He had that intensity about him. Did not go with the voice I had heard on the phone either I thought as it had sounded sweet. Dressed rather nice for a Teacher though. Not a suit and tie type after all as I had seen him in a suit but he never had a tie! Liked an open collar it seemed. Looked good on him and he looked no more then forty but I was sure he was in his fifty's. No idea what he taught though. No idea then how he knew it was me that had called either but he came straight to my small table making me nervous and sitting across from me stuck out a hand. Should have said something very important to me but I was just so damn desperate. His voice deep but sounding relieved and the same voice as on the phone. That he did not even bat an eye at my appearance should have said loads to me! "Hi! I'm Professor Murphy. You must be Mallory?" Yes I had told him my name and that I was a student at the school. Never dawned on me then he may have just looked me up in the student registry or even run a background check on me. Should have thought of that I know but I was too messed up! Well he was leaving me both his home and Pet to care for, for a week or so after all. Was not thinking straight or I would have understood. If rolls were reversed I sure as hell would have run a check but I was so messed up I was amazed I could even remember my own name. Everywhere I looked I saw only my certain and horrible death! Mostly I was wondering all day if anyone would actually bother to come to my funeral! If they found the body. Yes I had accepted my imminent death! Ready to give up and die? Not sure on that but I was tired of fighting. Heard freezing to death was not painful. So tired of the pain.

However! I will tell you this much. He knew exactly who I was for quite a while! Knew about lots of things! About me! Had video surveillance on me even! Here at the Cafe as well! Not the only one he was watching but the one he hoped would call. Card had only been up a half hour before I got here. He had chosen me and set me up.

Totally confused by this turn of events I spluttered. "Y-Y-Yes, I'm Mallory." Shook his hand automatically. It was the polite thing to do after all and I always tried to be polite. One less thing they could hurt me with you see? He had a firm but nice handshake and seemed genuinely happy to shake mine. Problem here however was I had to go potty now! After that blast of cold air he let in when he came in. Not to mention being so nervous and one and a half large cappuccinos. Had been holding it for a while and I realized too long. Afraid I would be in the potty and if whoever showed up did not see me they would just leave, so I held it! Was on my second jumbo cappuccino as well. He must have noticed me squirming as he sat so he said so sweetly. "Please go use the potty if you have too Miss. It's okay. I'll wait." He had a pleasant smile and his eyes sparkled.

His smile was all sweet and genuine still when I got back and he launched right into it. He seemed so honest here. Was sort of. Only half of what he said was a lie. There was concern and compassion in his voice and that was real. "You really are a miracle, Mallory! Frankly I had already given up any hope thinking it too late when you called. Hearing your voice asking for the job made me so happy you understand. Thought I would have to stay home yet again this year. So very seldom do I get a chance to travel and see things so I jumped at this opportunity when it became available thinking it would be easy to find a House-Sitter. Those darn expensive airline tickets are non refundable as well it seems." He said now more upbeat sounding. Like he was really looking forward to his vacation. "Going to Greece finally. See the Parthenon! Never been there but it always looks so beautiful and I've always wanted to go for so long. My flight is scheduled to leave at seven tonight I'm afraid and I had given up Hope of making it. Been packed for a week with my bags in the trunk of my car just praying for someone to call. It would be utterly irresponsible of me to leave my poor Dogs alone that long! They would be okay unless there was an accident but what would people think of me if they found out?" He blushed with some embarrassment. Not what I expected at all here. Something about him made me trust him quickly however. He just seemed so? Well lost! Felt like a stray Dog himself. Yeah I'm sure that most victims of serial killers thought the same thing but I already expected to die so what the hell? "I really wish I could take you out there and show you the house properly and introduce you to the Boys but I would miss my plane as I have too board earlier then that. The Boys are big Babys but sweethearts so you will be fine. There is a lot of food there so help yourself to what you want. I'll give you half the money up front so you can buy any supplys you may need on the way out. The house is terribly secluded however and if we get a heavy snow you won't be able to get in or out till it gets plowed so keep that in mind. Not sure if my plow guy has his truck fixed yet! Hope you don't have to go out at all you see but I understand things come up. Please, I don't mind a visitor or two but I would prefer none. You know how it is? Bad enough I'm trusting you and I have no idea who you are." Nodded at him. That made sense to me! Lots of students would throw party's and stuff if they had the chance I knew. Was however an utter lie! See all the pieces were there though but I just never put them together. Probably just did not care! Well I just wanted to live! "There are a bunch of emergency and contact numbers on the buffet in the front hall. If you have to get out and snow is deep just call the plow guy and he will come if he can. He bills me so you don't have to worry about anything. It's really a big house and I use very little of it so sleep wherever you want." Confused did not cover how I felt then. Felt like Dorthy caught in that tornado but saw a chance! Felt actual hope! Did not want to die! Knew the old adage if it looks too good to be true it probably isn't good! If I had a real choice I would have turned him down and run out of there but freezing in my car was no option now was it? Hated myself and my life but I did not want to die! Wanted something good! Knew there had to be something better somewhere! Okay, I actually felt safer in a way with it this way. If he was not coming with me he could not rape and kill me till he got back! Thought maybe if I did a real good job for him and he did not plan on killing me maybe he would be so grateful he would be able to help me out somehow when he got back. Was a Professor after all. Hope and Depression can exist in the same place! He slid a thick envelope and some keys across the table smiling so nicely. "Thank you very much Mallory. You'll be just fine now but I really have to run if I want to catch my flight. I trust you!" He sounded like he did. Maybe I should not have trusted him so much. Then again maybe I should have trusted him more. He shook my hand again and left quickly.

     Sure I was in shock! What had just happened here? Had not even said I would do it but he just assumed I would. Had not said much really as he did all the talking. True he may have realized I was looking for somewhere safe to hide from the looks of my face but? So weird! Picking up the envelope it was thick. Opened it and gasped as there was a lot of cash in there! This was just half? Several sheets of paper I assumed were instructions on stuff. One had the address of the house on it and I had a piece of shit, I mean car, so I tossed my empty cup and went to it. Had to ask directions a bit as I did not know the area well. Never batted an eye at him being so prepared as he had sounded desperate. Probably anal retentive. Certain he would have a washer and dryer living out there I went to the Salvation Army store and got a few clothes with the money. T-shits and sweat pants mostly. Might be some laundry in my trunk even. Dirty? Clean? No idea! Store for necessity's. Tampons and ice cream! Some frozen Pizzas as well. He did not strike me as the frozen pizza type. Yes I had counted the money and the envelope had five hundred dollars in it. He had said that was half. A thousand dollars to watch some Dogs for just over a week?! Well I always liked Dogs. They never judge! That he was willing to pay that much should have told me something though. Then again he never said how long he would be gone for?! The longer the better for me!

Turns out there were directions to the house in the big envelope though! Right on the back of the sheet that held his address! Felt like such an idiot after having asked the cashier at the cafe how to find the road. Looked at them at the gas station as I filled my tank. Directions on other things were in there like how to operate the coffee maker and some appliances. Pretty fancy stuff from the looks of the directions. Did not seem very hard to operate most stuff however so I kind of wondered. He was a Teacher after all and I knew some students needed directions to the toilet so it seemed like just that. Teaching is a hard habit to break I find. Is a habit too! Got gas for the car and myself and took the long drive outside the city in the dark eating my burrito. Almost the Winter Solstice after all and the sun was setting already. Mallory was already dead though and I just did not know it! Oh she was! The Professor murdered her! (Not in the Study with the wrench Steve!) Wait for it. Kind of complicated but I will explain as best I can. Mallory was going out there to that house but she would never leave!

Into the huge National Forest I went. Not hard to find the place however it turned out as the address was posted well on the sturdy looking mail box out by the road. Heavily protected from snow plows as well. Could not see the house from the road with the thick snow covered trees however so I went up the very long driveway cautiously. DAMN! Secluded did not come close! Had not seen another house in miles on the main road. Hell the driveway was almost a mile long. Than I saw his house! Sure you could call it a house. The term Mansion comes to mind as well. Not a big one mind you. Kinda got a Gone With the Wind vibe from it. One of those big southern colonial houses you know. With space for the large family and the slaves and servants? Beautiful home! Definitely a dozen bedrooms at least. Mighty big and expensive looking for a Teacher. Safe however! No way could he find me out here.

Pulled up right by the front doorway and parked. Not sure where else too. With the layer of snow that could be lawn and not parking spots. Below freezing outside so I knew the food would be okay but I grabbed the bag of clothes and tampons. Would need them soon it felt. Cramps were getting worse and my Period was ready to start. No sense standing in the cold thinking about it. Time to go in and meet his Dog! Pulled the key and unlocked the door. It was late and pretty dark already so the gloom inside the house was very deep as I went in. Could barely make out any shapes! Went in to the warmth and shut the door to the cold quick pulling my coat off fast as I felt the heat envelope me. Heater in my car was not very good so I was cold by the time I got here. Had to grope for the light switch in the near dark though. Heard something big sounding moving in the dark behind me! Stayed calm however. Must just be the Dog. He had not said how big it was had he? Had not said anything about it! Or much else for that matter I realized! Had figured he was more the miniature Poodle type! Yippee! Found the light switch. Flicking it on I began to turn and was suddenly hit hard by something dark and massive driving me to the floor hard screaming. SHIT! He had said DOGS I quickly Remembered! Nothing about freaking Moose though damn it! There were three of them! Moose that is and they apparently liked the sound of people screaming I think as they were on me fast. The thing about screaming is you have to open your mouth to do it and these Dogs were not only kissers but apparently very French. Some of you know what I mean. Big Dog tongue in the mouth is weird. Not bad mind you but very different. Got my throat scraped for free however. Could cross that off my to do list! The second one apparently very disappointed he could not get in my mouth as well violently stuffed his snout in my crotch hard and made me yelp. Tongue came out of my mouth and it instantly just sat on my chest looking down at me and WOOFED! This is normal Moose/Canine behavior I am told! Not sure I buy it. Not normal Moose you see! My hands however were kinda pinned beneath it's backside and I could not move it for the life of me. Now I am not light but he still outweighed me it felt. Definitely a he too. Could see that all to well from here. Bigger balls then Asshole had. Cuter too. Of course that would not b hard. Yes I am kinda pudgy with nice breasts and red hair but this thing weighed more then me I was sure so I had to lay there and squeal as the other two snorted my crotch for a while! Once again, it was not unpleasant just shocking. Apparently my begging skills needed improvement as they were not listening.

    Expected Chihuahuas and found Moose! Friendly Moose sure but still Moose! Problem was I did not speak Moose and they did not seem to understand English! Yes I tried a Cockney accent! Saw his name tag as he drooled on me. Catching my breathing I said. "Hi Apollo! I'm Mallory!" Maybe they knew Greek? He went WOOF! Slurp! My face was at least clean now. Hurt more but I was sure the dried blood was gone now. This was not what I expected in the least but you know? I sorta liked it! So affectionate. Too affectionate? Got none of that in my life! Huge house, so huge Dogs! Made sense to me now. Apollo wasn't too fluffy but a beautiful brindle color. Personally I always preferred big Dogs. More to cuddle. Always afraid I'd break a little Dog if I held it tight! These Moose were serial rapists however it seemed. Felt quite violated now as they had fun in my crotch! Still not unpleasant but extremely intense. Glad I still had pants on!

Grew nervous about when they would let me up however as all three were sitting on me now and I already had to pee from the cold outside. Yes I have a small bladder. Being crushed by Big Dog at that moment did not help any. Fancy heavily polished wood floor however so I was not too worryed if I had an accident but still. Talking to them sweetly I asked, no I begged them to get up. "Please Boys! I need to tinkle! Get off so I can get up." Their response? Not really what I wanted. Apollo just farted on my chest! In my cleavage! A real hot one too. Stunk big time! Warmed me a bit sure, but it was seriously gag worthy? Twenty minutes later I was totally begging them to get up but they seemed to be getting more comfortable. They laid down instead. On me! Not sure about the Professor but the Moose sure intended to keep me it seemed! Probably just found me very comfortable! Was a bit squishy so I understood that one. The intense pressure however had been building up inside my bladder all that time and their weight only made it worse so I knew I was not going to make it much longer. So with a sigh I finally just gave up. Clothes needed washing anyway. Had to be a mop here somewhere too. With a sigh I just let it go and My jeans grew hot with golden liquid quite rapidly. Had to go bad! Wetness spreading fast between my legs. Dogs began sniffing hard quickly as it puddled under my rump however. Had to go really bad so it was a puddle. The two on my legs got up and I watched, quickly telling them. "NO!" In total horror as one of them just lifted his leg and peed all over mine! The second did the same only he got it right in my crotch so our urine rapidly mingled beneath me. Kinda liked that idea for some strange reason. Just felt so connecting. So bonding. Not the first time I had been pissed on but definitely the nicest! Apollo got up and off of my chest finally so once able too I sat up fast.

Paying no attention to the Dogs around me I was looking only at the wetness of my pants and the puddle beneath me in horror. Was shocked by what they had just done to me! Shrieked loud as I felt hot liquid on my back suddenly. Twisting to see Apollo behind me with his leg lifted peeing on me my boobs got wet too! Glad I had my coat off at least! Did not know Dogs or Moose were into wet T shirt contests! No bra on either so my nipples showed well through the wet material. Getting up in momentary disgust all three Dogs went rapidly to where my urine was still puddled on the floor and began licking it up wildly. Leaving them to it in disgust I went looking for a shower upstairs. Not thinking about much else however I forgot to grab the bag of clothes before I went up. The stairs were just off the front hall and I could make them out in the gloom! Found no light switch so I just went up. As I went up the stairs however the lights came on. Motion sensors? Very high tech house.

Now I can't say I was actually mad really as I went up. Should have been! Still they were just Male Dogs and very friendly Male Dogs. Acting like Male Dogs do. Well I was new here and knew it could have been worse. Much worse! In spite of what the Professor said I was a stranger in the house and they may have attacked me. A small dog would most likely hide. These Boys could have killed me easily. Okay they did actually attack me but they could have tried to hurt me bad if they were scared. Love however can kill as well! The Professor must have lots of faith in his Moose. Like I said I was expecting a small lap Dog! Knew about Male Dogs and their obsessive peeing on things as I had walked many to help pay to get here so I understood Male Dogs did this thing to mark their territory. Usually not on people but I was sure I was now their territory. Kinda like a sorority initiation! Only nicer. The storys I heard at college already! Kinda wondered if it meant I was a part of their Pack now as my momentary disgust faded and they would accept me better now. If so it was really a rather sweet gesture I thought. Flattering even. Meant they liked me and wanted me to join them! Had seen no aggression in them yet. Just huge Moose like exuberance!

That Asshole I had run from? He tied me up naked and gagged me in the shower stall in November for Thanksgiving Weekend and he had a four day party in our apartment. Had been on my period then and told him I did not have the energy to do a party. So I watched them all come in and piss and shit for the first two days from where I was tied. Many finally peed on me that second night. Well after the first one did it because another person was shitting they all saw it as a challenge. The Girl he had fucked that weekend numerous times came in each morning just pushing me down and then she would piss and shit on me! Telling me as she did what her and Asshole had done in my bed and how great it was in detail. Got puked on a few times as well. These Dogs peed on me because they liked me and wanted me to be one of them! No doubt there. Made all the difference in the world. Kinda felt sweet to me. Pants felt kind of cold and wet though. Did not want to ruin his furniture or I may not have actually changed so fast. No one else seemed to like me. My whole life! These Boys did.

Something about it in my head made me think that! It was quite sweet I thought. They had not been mean in the least! Just playful from what I saw. Which is probably why I was smiling when I found his bedroom with it's large attached bathroom. Put my wet clothes in the sink and getting naked I got in the shower. Oh it was a nice big shower tub. Had not had a bath in a long time! Would be nice to soak in this later. Still sore in spots from my beating and I thought it may ease the aches. The shower was nice and the hot water lasted. Such soft plush towels too! The Professor had money, that was for certain! Maybe inherited or he won the lottery. Had no idea. Knew he could not afford this luxury on a Teachers salary! Did not matter to me either then. What did matter was I finally realized I had not brought the clothes up. Could always just walk through the house naked but I was bashful for some reason. Went to his closet in desperation and found an older looking, well worn, red flannel button down shirt and put it on. Covered my bottom well it was so long so I didn't worry about pantys for now. Not wearing his underwear! Even clean I was not going that far. Did not want to even know if he wore boxers or briefs! Frankly that felt like I was going too far so his drawers were off limits. Wrapped my clothes in the towel and went down in search of the laundry room. Towel needed washing too as I had finally started my period I saw as it had red smears on it. Forgot the Tampons in the car! Well I thought I put them in the bag with the clothes! Just have to wait till my clothes were washed as I was not going out like this! Damn cold out there. Would lock myself out with my luck and the Professor would come home and find my frozen body on his steps. Grabbed the clothes I brought in so I could wash them as well. May as well, right? Was running the washer anyway. Give them a wash as well. Why waste the water. Still not a full load either. Nice washer dryer combo he had. Frankly, wearing his shirt meant all my clothes got washed! That was a plus!

This house is fantastic I thought the whole time. Well what I had seen of it. Huge kitchen with an island like thick wooden cutting board in the middle. Lots of gadgets on plentiful counter space. My kind of kitchen with a mix of old and new. Nice big old wooden table there in the middle as well. The Dogs three dishes were in there against the cupboards with a larger water dish with a hose into it. Must be automatic looking that way I thought. Definitely cool! Another much thicker tube hung down from a large square metal box on the counter. This tube was almost the size of a car wash vacuum hose and I wondered what it was for. There were names on the dishes but no Dogs and I wondered where they went. Apollo, Fenrir, and Cerberus. Recognized the names! Meant he was probably an English Lit. Teacher with names like that I thought rolling my eyes. There was a huge Moose door I mean Doggy door in the back door. Probably fit a Moose through it! Looking out the window above it I saw a large fenced in area. Bigger than Assholes apartment had been! Tall fence too I thought. Eight feet at least! Lots of things in the woods for Doggys to chase so I understood that. These Dogs were well thought of that was certain. Found the laundry room at last, right off the kitchen where it should be I guess. Had cleaning supplys in there as well. Remembering my puddle I grabbed a mop after starting the washer and went to the entrance hall to clean the pee off the floor. Not much left really so I was quick! That done at least I left the mop and went exploring while clothes got washed. Still no sign of the Moose, I mean Dogs! Well I was sort of worried about another sneak attack. Or would that be a sneak cuddle?

Thought I was lost and just going in circles when I found a room with low lights on that seemed to be the study or den. Not sure what else you'd call it. This room looked very lived in. Beat up but very comfortable looking couch, large wooden desk, large screen TV on the wall across from it, shelves of books just everywhere, and three huge Dog beds along the wall next to the door I had come in. Knew the Professor spent a lot of time in here now as this room looked quite lived in. Still no Dogs though which I thought was a good thing. Liked Dogs and all but these guys were just a bit much at the moment. Way to excited. Had no pantys on yet either! Cold nose on bare ass would probably make me scream and I knew how much they liked screaming! Way to big to be lap Dogs but I was sure they thought they were Lap Dogs! Wondered if it was just my being new to them or if they always did this with visitors. Never thought it was actually neither of those! Would never have guessed the truth in a million years! Sure I was set up but the Professor did not know everything! Only a slight miscalculation but it had major consequences. The little details are the most dangerous as they have a way of causing drastic change in the best plans! Seemed very friendly at least I thought. Not one growl out of them earlier after all. Excited whimpers? Oh yes!

Speak of the Devil though! Turned to leave when the other door almost opposite the one I came in pushed open and they came in. There were two doors in here almost opposite each other like I said and they had no handles as they kinda swung. For the Dogs I assumed correctly. Did not see into the room they had come from as I was not in a good position any more. All three huge Dogs stood there looking at me seriously cocking their heads and sniffing. Apollo was actually the smaller of the three. He was the brindle. The other two a bit bigger and shaggier. One had long light brown, black, and white fur like a Saint Bernard. Probably was one or at least a mix. The other a dark brown almost black Monster made me think of a large Mastiff but extremely furry. A Woolly Mastiff! Noticed right away they did not look so friendly anymore! Not scary or anything just not happy. No tongues were hanging out! No happy Doggy smiles! All three were sniffing a bit like Dogs do so I thought nothing of it. Apollo suddenly cocked his head to the other side like he was actually thinking. Yeah and about eating me I was suddenly sure! Well that was what came in my head at the moment and I got nervous fast. "Never show fear!" You hear them say that all the time. My ass! At least two outweighed me, maybe all three. These were unnaturally big Moose! Did not scream yet but I began backing up quickly. Thinking I actually was going toward the door behind me however as they came forward I did not try and look. Very dumb of me. Not menacing me at all really but I was scared in a way still. Not wild and happy like they were before you see. Kinda curious perhaps, it felt. They were only sniffing the air. Maybe they were not sure what I was doing in this room? Their beds were in here so that made sense to me. Maybe they thought I was invading their space and going to steal their chew toys! Made me nervous still so I spoke. "Hi fellas. Just looking around. Beautiful house. Nice beds you have." My tone was kept gentle and soothing trying hard too keep any fear out of it. "You are very pretty Boys too... Yoaargh!" Missed the door by two feet and found one of the Dog's beds. Went down in one backwards and hard on my butt. They came at me fast now! Too fast? Thought maybe they just wanted to play again as they looked excited finally. Well I hoped that was it.

Knew I was completely wrong and in trouble fast as my legs were shoved apart by a huge Canine head and shoulders and a cold wet nose began snorting my still bare vagina wildly! It was Apollo again. Suspected he was in charge. Rapidly I began scooting backwards on my back sort of Crab walking till I hit the wall with my head. Got maybe two feet! As soon as I stopped going backwards I was pressed to the floor and had the dark ones large leathery balls on my lips and my nose was up in his smelly butthole as he sat smack dab on my face! Fluffy butt!

Right on it though! Dark under there as he was fluffy. He was most definitely heavier then me! His strong musky aroma, not totally unpleasant, rapidly filled my nostrils when suddenly he went. PFFT! Oh he stunk! That was nasty! Farted right up my nose and immediately I tried to gag! Big mistake on my part however. Got a big warm leathery Doggy testicle in the mouth when I opened it to gag you see. Had worse in my life so I did not panic yet. Stay calm! They were not trying to hurt me! Had no doubt they could if they actually wanted too! The other fluffy one lay across my chest fast and was pinning my arms down. He was the biggest! Well heaviest! Not sure I could have moved the one on my face even anyway. Gasping hard as something wet pushed into my vagina against my clit so I sucked the Dog nut further in my mouth. My choice was a simple one and I knew it. Suck Dog ball or snort Dog poop! No third option here! Honestly however his testicle was nice in my mouth! Guys Pubic hairs are so wiry and course so they are irritating. Because they won't use conditioner down there! Hell most guys don't even wash it! His very sparse ball hair was quite soft like the rest of his luscious fur. Not the first testicle I had in my mouth but by far the nicest. Apollo was absolutely and savagely having his way with his tongue in my Pooter the whole time, which is extremely distracting I assure you and I kept gasping around Doggy Harbles. Seems they truly wanted to eat me after all! Liked being eaten this way better but they were Dogs! That was wrong! Right? Their tongues are wider, thicker, and stronger than a humans. And I would be lying if I said that what the Dog between my legs was doing did not feel good! Okay! It was kinda beyond good as his tongue pressed so hard and rapidly on my clit sending waves of pleasure ripping through me. Better then I ever had before! No one had ever eaten me out like this before. So rough, intense, savage and yet still loving! He wanted to taste it all! Yes I groaned a bit which apparently felt really good to the one with a testicle in my mouth. Building to an actual orgasm quite rapidly I was Huffing Dog Butt and good. Always liked a tongue down there you see and he had a big, long, strong one! Knew about some people having sex with Dogs. Never much interested me. Kinda scared me in fact as I had seen how big some Dogs penises are. What I had seen on line mostly looked boring for the Dogs as the Girls just masturbated with them as well. Could not move now so they could have their way with me all they wanted and I could not stop them! Knew any of these Dogs could kill me by themselves! So I would do what I had too to survive. Had seen Wolves kill on nature shows and it is not pretty. Did not want to die that way! Oh they may not kill me sexually but they were big Dogs and more then capable of killing a person if angry! Even if I called 911, help was over thirty minutes away! No idea where a phone was either. Did wonder what the Professor had taught these Dogs or exactly what went on here as I was used. They seemed to know what they were doing so well too. Was this something they did all the time to the Professor's guests? Sacrifice them to his Dogs? Pretty sure I was going to be raped soon! Not the first time I was raped either! Had been raped several times in my life! Was not scared now however like all the other times. Most rape is a power struggle and the Girls get hurt because it excites the twisted Loser! These Dogs meant me no harm what so ever. Just horny Boys wanting sex. And after those three major orgasms I was ready for anything. Believe me!

Knew deep in my heart without a doubt these Boys would do whatever they wanted with me anyway and I was helpless to stop them! Rape me like I was just a Back Alley Bitch in heat! Even if I could find a weapon I knew how to use I could not stop all three before I died horribly. Could not outrun them if I tried and if I got outside I would freeze to death! Not even sure where my keys were at the moment. They did not want to hurt me either it seemed and I knew I did not want to hurt them. Surrendering my body was the only real choice here. Fought hard not to cry here accepting my fate! My mouth was full of warm Dog ball still after all. Nice leathery texture. Very interesting. Stuffed up nose however might mean no more Dog butt smell but little or no air either. They may not want to hurt me but could kill me just as quickly by accident! So to distract and calm myself I began sucking Big Dog nut gently trying to get into it by imagining it was Brad Pitt and enjoy myself. Was very enjoyable too once I stopped worrying and relaxed. Just tried to pleasure the Boy I was with Dog or not. Began to hum and he whimpered. Well I came again! Made the Dog on my face Whimper when I did. PFFT! He farted again! Oh God! Gasping as a big tongue went inside me at that instant I got a lung full of smelly Dog fart. Kind of a musky smell to it really. Mixed with sewage. Smelled worse many times in my life that's for sure!

My fourth orgasm was a strong loud one and the big Boy on my face enjoyed it so much his body trembled. Felt the shirt I wore pop open as buttons gave way and the one laying on me was licking my bare tits with his massive tongue quickly. Took a moment to realize my arms were free and I quickly grabbed the one on my face. Did not try and push him off though I am ashamed to admit. Too late for that! Oh I was horny as all hell now and really enjoying myself! Holding the dark one there and pulling him tighter on my face I knew I was getting my nose further up in his tooter. Had issues with sex in many ways, for good reason, and kind of went on automatic all the time. Was that way now mostly. If you can't love the one you want, love the one your with! My feet had wrapped up over Apollo's shoulders and back hooking my ankles I realized. Gone in my orgasm induced lust! Had eaten or drank nothing since getting here or I would have strongly suspected drugs of some kind! Would really be nice to have something to blame it on you understand but I knew the truth! This insatiable desire I was feeling was all mine. These Dogs were really being very sweet to me and I loved it as most guys were just mean. Putting my pleasure first it seemed! They sure wanted to please me! Not used to that you see! This felt just WOW! Lost in the joys of Doggy induced ecstasy I caved!

Wanted more! That was scary to realize. You will understand in time. Did not stop me from wanting it however! Worked harder at pleasing my Man, I mean Dog! Wanted to give them what they had given me! Had gentle passionate sex once in my life! All the others were rather disappointing and unsatisfying at best! Usually extremely painful!

Not easy for me to do but by God I got the second large Dog testicle in my mouth filling it completely! Knowing for sure now I would only be able to breath through my nose which was still in this Dog's hot soft tooter I prayed he did not have to poop.

During sex or while very horny you will most likely do things you never would otherwise! Had as well at times but never thought I would go this far! Things you would normally not enjoy can be pleasant as well. Spanking, anal, and other stuff. Figured it was the orgasms causing it but those farts were suddenly sort of growing very tolerable. Almost enjoyable? Definitely hot in my nostrils! Slid my hand down the Dog's furry chest and onto his belly finding his furry sheath. His cock sheath was so unbelievably soft furred I sighed at it. But what was inside it was hard as a rock by now. So big too! Gasped as I found the bulb! Oh my God! It was huge! Of course I thought it would tear me up when he put it in so I hoped it did not go that far. That I even thought of him putting it in me was shocking. Knew they would not be happy till they got something from me however so I began stroking this big Boy's rock hard mighty cock in the sheath. Well that's my story! So

I had accepted my weird situation and kinda lost myself in it. Focusing only on my pleasure and pleasing them now. Not easy to do but I had practice. Never fun practice though. Not enjoyable like this. Could easily and gladly give them all hand jobs I thought. I blame multiple orgasms.

Groaned hard as a fifth orgasm racked my body making me whimper around big, hot, soft Dog nuts snorting up his tooterhole, getting a whimper out of him. Stroking harder the sheath eventually slid off of him but grudgingly. Tight fit as it was huge. My fingers wrapped tightly around his massive Dog Bone. Bigger then anything I ever had in my hand or anywhere else for that matter. It was kinda slimy with its own lubrication but so warm and smooth. Hard as a rock however. The sheath did not go down over the bulb but it did not have too! From bulb to tip it was longer and thicker then any cock I ever had! At least eight inches. Felt liquid of some kind splashing my arm rather quickly as I stroked it. Not lots and I knew how long Dogs got stuck together! Had to assume it was more a precum like lubricant than ejaculate but I knew I had Dog semen on me! Yes I found I even wondered how it tasted, lost in the throws of my desire! You ever have insane thoughts while having sex? Have you ever had sex? My other hand was running through the fur of the one on my chest quite lovingly. He was soft and very fluffy. My crotch was going up to meet Apollo's amazing tongue now. The one getting the nice hand job on my face whimpered well his joy as he squirted more all over me. Wanted to make him a very happy Boy now! Yes I admit it! This was what I always thought sex should be like! Not necessarily with Dogs but mutually pleasing and just pure enjoyment! Proud now that he was shooting his seed on me it seemed!

Suddenly Apollo barked in my vagina and my whole body shuddered with that sensation! That was so totally intense. The big Boy quickly got up off my face pulling his nuts from my mouth with an audible POP! Shocked with myself as I could not stop trying to pull him back down. Maybe it was an aerosol drug?! Was the house full of cameras like on one of those stupid TV shows? Was I going to be an Internet sensation? My mind was reeling in such absolute horror as all the Dogs moved away from me. Not why I should have. Were they done with me? Brain was hopeful for that but the body was an entirely different story all together! Rolling to my hands and knees I just lunged like a Dog for the Dark one whose tag read Fenrir! Wanted my balls back you see! Well I did and I am not ashamed to tell you that! Orgasm induced insanity sounds like a good defense to me. Knocked him over and rolled him onto his back. His thick veiny cock still exposed I got a good look at it's magnificence. Was not done with those nuts! Apollo was apparently not done either and was on me from behind fast, growling and snarling while mounting me like I was just a Bitch. Maybe temporary insanity! Opening my mouth I took Fenrir's still very hard and exposed cock in my mouth for a taste, sucking. Looked kinda cool all red and veiny and I wanted a taste so bad I had no control. He woofed and I went deep not bothered by the slightly metallic taste at all. Apollo tore my skin and the shirt with his sharp dew claws as he wrapped his fore-paws around me thrusting so hard. Oh it hurt at first but I was beyond pain with my unquenchable lust now! It will do that you know! Endorphins are the best pain killer ever. He poked at my behind for a moment with his hard stiff cock and I found myself disappointed as it felt not so thick. Kept poking around, almost hitting my tooterhole and I was thinking it would not work. Then hitting the right spot he just slammed his Maleness into me deep and hard over and over rapidly tearing my pussy slightly with his rapidly swelling Dog-Cock. Grunted rapid fire with the force of each thrust. Maybe I whimpered. Never before had I been fucked so brutally and savagely yet with such tremendous desire and passion! Nor pleased so well!

The sensation was so very intense as I felt his cock and bulb swell inside me while still rubbing, rough but highly pleasurable. Quickly I was heading for a major vaginal orgasm from Apollo's cock as I slurped greedily on this huge thing in my throat. The slight metallic taste filling my mouth. "Take me like the BITCH I am!" Gagged it out with Dog-Cock in my mouth. Not easy! Oh I was out of control and out of my head. Lost in the powerful lust and moment I felt. Most likely insane but had so many reasons for that if it were. Not in my right mind most of the day thinking only of how I would die! Watch out what you wish for though they say. Had not come close to imagining what would kill me! One after another they had a go at my swollen throbbing pussy and I stayed on all fours for them whimpering my pleasure like a back alley Bitch in heat, my arms and legs trembling. Lost in my desires and madness!

Gladly being their Bitch!

Two words. Twelve Orgasms!

By the time Cerberus was on me and in me my body was just shaking with such intense pleasure. His cock however was a monster like him! Realized I was licking Fenrir's asshole at some point but did not stop. Did not care if he didn't? Rational human mind was locked in the closet I think. This was pure raw animal lust and when they growled at me I found I growled back! They liked that it seemed.

These Dogs swelled so much inside me I thought I would burst and the pleasurable feeling in me was so intense. A blur of pure sensation. Knew I was drooling like just a Bitch and did not care. Had Doggy drool on my back! Cerberus was just a total slobber factory! Letting go of my humanity I barked and howled just like one of them! They got even happyer at that. Felt so free inside at that moment as well! It was Amazing! My fears were gone for the moment. Replaced by ecstasy. Then once Cerberus came out and off I sighed with relief thinking it done.

Relaxed too soon it seemed as Fenrir jumped on my back and began poking away getting his turn in. Could honestly do nothing to prevent what was happening, could barely stay up, and Damn it, He deserved a turn! Knew it was coming and just locked my arms and legs as my strength was waning. My scream was a howl as he entered me. Right up my ass! God that was intense! Growling and barking on me in joy he went to town in my tight tooter hole! Owning it and me! It was all I could do to stay up and keep my face off the floor. Knowing full well how big he would swell I knew I was his for a while. It was not coming out of that hole till the swelling went down or there would be much pain and lots of blood! Wanted it to stay for a while any way I realized. Not afraid of the blood or pain you see. Kind of used to that. Wanted to Feel like a real "Bitch" that's all!

Do not judge me yet! The other two Boys started playing tug a war with the shirt I sort of wore still. Barely noticed as they ripped it apart and off making me naked like them. Okay I was wearing a fur coat still! It was finally too much for me as he actually made the tie and I felt the darkness take over as I passed out from my ecstasy. No idea how many orgasms I had but there were many. Passed out with big Dog-Cock up my throbbing tooterhole! Pleasant dreams.

CHAPTER 2 STRUGGLES Thursday December 20th

Confusion screamed in my head as I slowly began to wake up. Pain was still prevalent deep in my body! Not as bad as yesterday though it seemed. The deep scratches on my sides hurt the most. Sorta had many now. Between my legs was sore but also felt so nice. Butthole was still throbbing as well. Belly felt like heck where He had punched me so much the other night but not as bad now. Definitely was hungry however! Knew last night had been no dream at least however! Dry Dog cum was caked on my inner thighs after all. Kinda liked that feeling though. In the fetal position I apparently fit well in the Dog bed though. No idea how I got in it. One of the fluffy Dogs was laying on me keeping me warm at least. Ooh so warm! The other two pressed to my sides and I felt warm inside as well. Memory's and details flooded back and I was in total shock again! My God! What had I done last night? Could not believe I had done any of that! How I felt such shame. Shut up HooHa!

My blanket was awake and began licking my butt now! Well his head was at that end. Knew that as his leathery Harbles rested on my ear. Felt darn nice but I felt something else and I only whimpered my need. My blanket got off me quickly like he understood what I meant. Tried to stand but was knocked back down fast by one of them. Gentle still but knocked down. The Dog had a point however as my legs were so shaky still from last night I would have probably fallen and hurt myself. Still? Not sure that was their thinking I wondered. Was I a prisoner here? Was I watching the Dogs or were they the ones watching ME?! Was really wondering now as my mind raced in some extremely weird directions. Trying to go on all fours the Dogs did nothing bad to me. Just walked along beside me, pressing me, guiding me. Was so out of it still I did not even notice where we were headed till we were there. The Kitchen! That huge Doggy door was there. Did he know I had to go potty and this was his solution? He was pushing me that way! Tried to turn away and quickly I found myself slammed with a high check against the nearest cupboards being snarled at viciously in the face. Those were big teeth! Seemed more stern than angry to me however so I did not freak. Took a step experimentally toward the outside and he relaxed. Strange? Did they see me as one of them for some reason? Okay they may have had many reasons. Being naked and having sex with them was high on that list. Thinking fast I felt I could do this if I had no choice. Did not seem to be a choice either. Just had to be quick! Be colder then anything I had ever done but if I was quick enough it would not be too bad. Right? May even numb some of my pains.

So I went out quick into the cold and snow hoping to just get it over with and realized, just my luck, we were having a blizzard! Bad one as well! This wind was harsh! Almost vicious! Making it just that much colder and I had goosebumps quick. Visibility was so very little in the dark as well. The snow biting into my skin hard stung fast. Going to squat quick this Dog shoved me harder, further out into the snow making me stumble. Over and over he pushed me out into the deep freeze. Was freezing myself! Mind was a whirl with chaos. My naked tits were dragging in the white stuff it was so deep and he just kept pushing. My nipples were so hard from the intense cold already they hurt lots. Oh that snow was so cold on my bare skin! So painful! He just kept pushing and I did not understand why. Shivering very quickly out here I knew I was in trouble. Snow was so deep already my ass would be in it when I squatted. Hell, it almost was now! Must have gotten close too a foot of snow. No choice! He had stopped pushing finally for some reason. Could barely see the lights in the house as I looked back. Shivering hard already, I gritted my teeth and hunched my back shoving my fat butt in the icy snow with a groan. Took way to long for my taste but finally I let loose with a sigh. Done I turned to the house but he blocked me again growling now. "Oh God I am going to freeze to death out here! Please let me go in!" Pleaded desperately with him and he growled even more at me. Apollo had come out I saw and I watched him shit while I shivered naked on hands and knees in the snow now crying. Maybe that was it? Maybe Fenrir wanted me to poop as well? Did not feel like it. Could always try! Rather numb you understand so it surprised me when I actually did in a rush. Dog-Cum enema! If I was warm it would have been a relief. Was a lot coming out! Could he actually smell it in me somehow? Dogs had amazing sense of smell after all. Were they that good? He came over and sniffed my poop well as I watched shivering waiting for his approval. Seemed satisfied with it as he lifted his leg on it. Yes I watched him pee on my poop. Had seen Dogs do it plenty of times but never paid much attention! Was interesting to watch when I did. He shoved me over to Apollo's poop pile roughly and then he sniffed it well. Fenrir was between me and the house still blocking me for some reason. On a hunch I too bent down and sniffed the Dog-Poop as well. Smelled worse in the Girl's Room in high-school. Yes Boys! Girl's shit stinks! Just not as bad as yours! Trust me on that one! He seemed satisfied with my behavior now though and turned to go in so I followed grateful. Twice he stopped in front of me quick though. Knew what he wanted somehow. He was a Dog! Not hard to figure out! So I was numb and shivering but I sniffed his furry butt well. Was he? Were they? Teaching me how to be a Dog? Sure seemed like it! Strange but what else could be happening here?

     Mind was kinda numb as well it seemed. Had I given up?

     Inside finally the warmth was shocking! All three Dogs were there in the kitchen. They pushed me toward a water filled dish somehow knowing I was very thirsty. They had not really hurt me yet but I had no doubts they could! Maybe they actually saw me as a new Dog and were teaching me the ropes and all! Sort of housebreaking me! Only thing I could come up with. Kind of cute in a way. Made sense in a weird way as well. Had to assume they were trained to go all the way out by the fence to potty and that was why I was pushed. Could not see the fence in the dark but the distance fit. Put my face down in the dish and drank from it. Cerberus stuck his muzzle down there by me and began lapping up water. Another lesson? Why not? Imitated him after watching closely. He curled his big tongue backwards and pulled up more water that way. Not easy with a human tongue but I tried. Had a long tongue but nothing like his. Is not nice, to not try and learn something if someone goes to the trouble of trying to teach you. Always learn new things!

Tried it but not very successfully really. Would take a lot of practice I thought but I would get it eventually. Realizing what I had just thought I tried to stand up and got knocked down again. Knew why! Professor Murphy would be back in two weeks?! Could I be a Dog for that long? They wanted me to be one and planned on forcing me if necessary! Maybe they thought I was trying to get on the counter? Definite no no for Doggys! Was I being a Bad Dog? Were they trying to keep me out of trouble? How sweet. Thought I could try and be a Dog for a while. Might freeze to death taking a dump if it got much colder. Just have to potty fast! Knew what I had to do out there now so I could be quicker I felt! Apollo pushed an empty food dish over to the device with the big tube that hung there getting close but not quite too the floor and he stepped on something by it I had not noticed. Saw him deliberately put a paw out on a small pad. The box growled and the dish filled with food from the tube. DOG FOOD! How ingenious! Looked like a mix of dry and wet foods however. Looked better then somethings they served me in high-school! The dish got pushed over to me. Right below my face! Oh crap! Thought. "Moment of truth!"

Looking at them I honestly tried. Could not bring myself to taste it. It was just too much! "Please? I can't...UGH!" Slammed me into the cupboards again! Had to know. "What is..." Slam! So I growled. Nothing! Barked. Again nothing. Started to speak again and wham into the cupboards. They did not want me to talk for some reason it seemed? Hard to focus but I thought maybe if they actually saw me as a Dog it really confused them when I spoke and they did not like that. Whimpered and rubbed on the two still here. Fenrir had left the room but the other two were still watching me. Not like I was not hungry! Had no idea when I had eaten last but it was not much. Why I was surprized I had pooped that much! The food in the dish looked disgusting for certain but I still lowered my head. Did not smell the greatest that was sure. Maybe some Salsa or Ranch dressing would help. Did not think Dogs were allowed in the fridge either however. Might be able to sneak something? There were three of them though! They could watch me at all times if they were serious. If this was all I was going to get to eat I may as well before they punish me again. Trying to breath only through my mouth I took a bite. A small one and they began to growl. Tasted nasty! Big bite! Don't chew! Just close my eyes bite and swallow. Just like a Dog! Was that why they ate that way? Again and again! Had not realized just how hungry I was till I found myself actually licking the dish clean. Had worse once or twice in my life. Maybe some Oregano or Cilantro would help! Well if I was eating it for a couple weeks maybe I could make it better.

Fenrir came in the room and walked up to me once I was done eating with something in his mouth. He dropped it on the floor in front of me. Looked down at it in Horror! It was an actual Dog collar! Beautiful and pink but a real DOG COLLAR! Not new. There was a tag on it even. The name on the tag was Athena. No other tags on there. The three Males all had licenses and rabies tags as well as one with their names and this address on it. Knew somehow, deep down, if I put the collar on I was definitely surrendering my humanity! What choice did I have? Only have be one of them till I was rescued after all and humanity is highly over-rated. Professor would come home and save me. Had been thinking a lot about this all morning. Was I willing to be a Dog? Act like one? Live like one? Better than a human punching bag that was for sure! Dogs in general always seem happy. These Boys were big but honestly gentle and friendly. Horny for sure but they were Boys! As I reached for the collar I saw my hands trembled.

Okay! Now I did not think they would kill me intentionally if I didn't put it on! Would not even hurt me bad! On purpose at least, but they had been very rough already and if they got angry or rougher an accident could happen. Broken bone? Possible internal bleed if they broke a rib smashing me into the walls. One might be broken now from the Asshole! Not even sure where the phones were in here as I had seen none yet. Mine was in my purse if I could find it. The way the snow was coming down they probably could not even get out here if I called. Was quite deep out there. If I lied about being hurt I would end up in jail as well. Did I really want anyone to see me like this? Better reason to put it on however? Knew if I went to either hospital or jail He would find out! Pretty sure he would finally just kill me when he found me.

Looking at each of the Dogs as they cocked their heads at me waiting for my answer expectantly I had to smile. The look on their faces was just so precious! Adorable Moose! They really liked me and wanted me to be a part of their family! Could see it in their eyes. Their Pack perhaps? Touching when I thought of it that way and very gladly I made my decision. With a sigh and a smile I put it on. They all barked happily at my action and I joined them in their joy barking back.

Quickly they all ate and than herded me back to the den where they all proceeded to make me their BITCH! Again! Expected that one this time however! Kinda hoped for it even. Yes I did! Not proud of it but I was rather horny for some reason. Had been since the time I got here. Stood pretty for them Boys this time wagging my butt like the Dog I now was. That's what I thought. Not even close yet! Headed there however. They took turns mounting me and fucking me hard! Those not fucking me took turns shoving their rumps in my face to be sniffed and I gladly sniffed too! They all had a unique smell I noticed after a few sniffs. Subtle, sure, but it was there. Except when they farted! Well, nothing was subtle then. Certain I could not recognize these smells elsewhere I knew they could. Dogs can actually smell cancer! Or a seizure before it hits!

It helped me to sense it better if I licked it, it seemed. The smell was better understood that way. They licked my tooterhole so I felt it only fair to lick theirs after all. Knew Dogs used scent markers and smelled each others butts. Not sure I could get that good but they were certainly trying to teach me their personal scents I realized! And how to be a better Dog too! My head was in such a weird place when I took the job. Well that is an understatement! Weirder place now! So I was willing. Well I could spend my holiday break learning to be a Dog! Had it's good points! Was certainly interesting! Always curious about everything. The way they kept mounting me and filling my vagina with their semen I was sure they were trying to teach me how to have Puppys! Got a chuckle out of that when I first thought it but kept going back to it throughout the day strangely. Brian fog! Think each had his cock in me twice! Felt so dreamy in my head. Felt funny since I got here! Maybe before? Had He hit my head against the wall too hard this time and done real damage? Found myself dreaming about having Puppys while I napped in a Dog-bed after sex. They completely wore me out so I slept well! In my dream I had eight Puppys. Had eight tits too. They were cute Puppys so I was a proud and happy Mama Dog!

Woke a while later surrounded by my three Boyfriends. They sure thought they were! Cerberus butt was in my face. He had just farted! Probably what woke me. Caught myself sniffing it subconsciously. Did not intend to but was and did not stop myself either! Just sniffed well. So tired of my humanity it seemed. Needed something much simpler it felt. Extracted myself carefully. They were asleep but I still stayed on all fours. Hey these floors were hard and I did not want to get slammed to them if I got caught. Kinda wobbly as well. Did not want to disappoint them Boys either I found. Was going to be hard to remember at times still I thought but for them if not myself I was certainly going to try. Don't forget my legs were quite shaky too. Let's see you get fucked for almost an hour or two and see how you feel the rest of the day! Had over a dozen orgasms that I remembered! All fours was definitely safer at the moment. So I made my way like that all the way to the Kitchen dreading what I was going to do.

Bracing myself I went outside fast! The snow was even deeper now but I went way out on hands and knees anyway. Thankfully at least the wind was down. Shivering fast I still went out to the fence before I squatted. AH! Wow I had to pee bad. Lots of yellow snow! He, he, he! Done I turned back toward the house. Fenrir was standing there not far away so I stayed where I was waiting. He came over sniffed and licked my pee then lifted his leg peeing right where I had! No idea what was expected of me I used all I knew of Dog behavior! Taking a guess I sniffed at his pee. He looked pretty happy about that. Licked his yellow snow as he had mine. Salty. He turned and let me catch up as we headed back in. Rubbed his body on me the whole way in too. Got a drink. Yes I was freezing but had warmed up quick enough last time so I was not worried. Remembered when I had a broken leg as a kid. That sucked! But it passed. This would to I was sure. Just had to be quick out there. The more I knew the quicker I could be! There were much worse things in my past but I tried so hard to never think of those. I'll get to them soon enough however and maybe you will understand. Yes it seemed like some sort of an ordeal like going out in the snow and I sure thought it was at first but as the day went on I realized these big Boys were quite affectionate with me in many ways. Rubbing. Licking. Just touching and being touched. Felt this was what a true family was supposed to be.

More affection from them then any one I had dated ever gave me. Not just the sex either! They genuinely wanted to be close to me. That I quickly realized usually broke out into piling on each other or wrestling however! Not real rough with me even if their claws did scratch me a bit. If I started bleeding they licked the wound for me till it stopped. Lots of butt sniffing happened all the time and not just mine I am ashamed to admit! When I understood it was a good thing and it made them happy when I sniffed theirs I did not hesitate when a furry butt got in my face. Sniff, Lick, Huff! If this was being a Dog, then I wanted to be a Dog for a while. Well being a human sucked!

Late in the afternoon we played chase! Which I completely sucked at. Trust me. Nowhere near as fast as them on two feet I did not stand a chance on hands and knees. It was kind of like tag! The second time I caught one, unaware it seemed, I realized they were letting me catch them so I pounced! Such wild joy and abandon in this I had not felt since at least a young child. Maybe never! My Childhood pretty much sucked!

Went out in the snow and peed again. They all came with me and peed as well. Freezing I still waited for them and both sniffed and licked their yellow snow before racing inside. It was still awkward but they let me get on hands and feet and go that way in a hurry. Faster then hands and knees! Got a drink and went quickly to the den. It was the warmest room I had found so far. Had no windows after all. Miraculously they understood I was cold and as I lay down in a bed they smothered me. Might just find me comfy! Got my face licked furiously and giggled like a little kid however. Felt such unbridled joy! First time ever!

We lay there a while. They dozed and I sorta thought. So far the Dogs had been in charge and I had just accepted what they made me do. Yes technically that meant they were raping me. Thought of that! Was not mean or vicious like the other times I had been raped. The sex I admit was just unbelievable however. They came out of the vagina easy with the bulb swollen but it was still just WOW! Last night when Fenrir had gotten me in the butt and gotten stuck it had been scary at the time certainly. Well I envisioned him tearing out of me and my colon falling out! Thinking about it now however I knew it had been rather pleasant and I was sorry I had passed out. Exciting in a very naughty way being stuck butt to butt. Well I had been an actual BITCH for a little while! Stuck on the end of His Dog-Cock! Thinking of this however I found I was getting myself horny.

Hey, my life was a mess. You ready for the nasty stuff yet? Here goes! Home had been Hell! Not like most people say their home was hell. Mine was! When I was ten my Father lost his job! So he was home a lot as he could not seem to get another job. Not sure he really tried. Which was odd even to me as many people loved him and he was quite popular around town! Really I have no idea if it was the stress that eventually broke him or if he was always just a sadistic prick and since he was working all the time we just never noticed it. See I have an older Sister and a little Brother. Dad slowly became increasingly violent a lot! Got worse when he drank. Smoked a lot too. Treated my pretty older Sister very nice but my Brother and me both got the belt! Often! Black eyes were not uncommon for me. That I started getting in fights at school to take out my anger made no one pay much attention to my injury's. Oh I got in fights too! Mostly with Boys much bigger then me. Was the only Girl I knew of who ever got a swirly in the Boys bathroom in middle school! Ten times!

Mom had become suddenly accident prone she would tell people to explain her visible injury's away. Looking back I think many knew but they liked my Dad so did not care. Mom was working an awful lot as well. Frankly I think more to be safe then we needed the money. She had three jobs!

Caught my older Sister with a cigarette one day when I was twelve. She was smoking it out back and I asked where she got the cigarettes. She said they were Dad's. So I threatened to tell him she had stolen his cigarettes thinking I finally had something to use on her. She just laughed in my face. Oh I was so young and naive. Had no idea yet! Way to young and naive to suspect what was going on. Told him about my Sister smoking his cigarettes to get her in trouble for once and he just hauled off and spit a big gob in my face telling me to leave my Sister alone or else and grabbing my wrist he burned me on the arm with his cigarette. Still have that scar. My Sister happily smoked in the house after that. Right in front of him. With him! Even lit her cigarettes for her like he was a Gentleman. He bought her her own Girly cigarettes after that and they were all buddy, buddy. He let her stay up very late on weekends all the time while Mom worked. My Sister made me go to bed at nine so her and Father could relax she said! Yes my Sister told me! She was in charge and I knew it! Even on weekends I went to bed early! Refused to go one night to push her back and Dad grinning ripped his belt off and held me down while She beat me bloody with it bare assed! When I turned thirteen and began to blossom so to speak things got worse. My tits began growing fast! Before long mine were bigger then my Sister's and that's when things began to fall apart fast. What I did not know is my Father and Sister were sleeping together! Yes I mean having sex! Had been for a while. Not sure when it started but I suspected when she was just eleven. Why he let her stay up with him! Had sex on the couch with her once we were asleep! If Mom was not coming home till morning she would sleep in his bed with him! No idea how it actually started between them or when! Do not want to either, but I know how it ended and I died. Oh I was dead! They had too revive me and restart my heart three times I am told.

You read that right! Well Mom was working a night shift double and would not be home till ten in the morning. By nine at night Dad was drunk and half naked in just his boxers saying he was hot. So was my Sister! Well she wore something very naughty of Mom's. He had started to let her drink at thirteen when Mom was away. She got so drunk that night however she passed out on the couch in a bad mood for some reason I did not understand. She had been treating me very nasty lately and when I complained to Mom once, my Dad quickly stuck up for my Sister lying for her and I would get beat once Mom was gone. By my Sister! He let her beat me with the belt badly at times the sadistic savage twat. He would hold me down and call me so many nasty things and worthless that I began to believe it. Why I let some psycho control me now. It was obvious looking back what was going on but I was young, naive, and living in a nightmare of fear. She had been sitting in Mom's chair when Mom was not home calling our Father by his first name or hunny. Daddy's little angel! If she did something bad she never got hollered at for it for a few years. Usually I did! She committed the crime but I did the time. My little brother withdrew and ran and hid all the time. While I was going to bed that night before she woke again Dad made a real lewd comment about me. It was only, "Shake that fine ass Girl!" But still! Was not only his Daughter but only thirteen! The way he said it, it was totally obscene! Still the only compliment I ever got from him! My Sister was already passed out or she would have flipped out with her jealousy then. You will see! Well I was blossoming and my breasts were already bigger then my Sister's. Took after my Mom! Her side of the family were mostly Cows! Dad's side was all small breasted. He was looking at me lately with lust and she saw! Her jealousy was terrible! About to pass the line between hate and murder!

His remark made me very nervous as I went to the bathroom quickly before bed. Never heard him come down the hall till he pushed open the bathroom door. It had no lock since Daddy kicked it in while coming after me and I tried to lock myself in one day a year or so ago. Quickly I tried to cover myself as I sat on the toilet and he grabbed my arm twisting hard. "Come on Baby. Show Daddy your sweet tits like your Sister does!" That shocked me then I saw his boxers were pulled down and his hard penis was already out! Shock and now sudden fear froze me momentarily at the sight. It was all he needed however and my nightshirt was yanked over my head fast and hard! Painfully as well. He was quite strong and yanked it off hard. He instantly groped a bare breast, mashing it hard, hurting me, as he moved till his penis was right there in my face! Actually touching my lips with it Oh God! This was bad! Very very BAD! Could not scream or he would shove it in!

That of course was when my drunk now fifteen year old Sister stormed in, having woken alone, screaming. "What the fuck is going on here?" She glared at us. "You filthy cheating Bastard! Trying to fuck my Sister instead of me?"

Father was a real shit! Could think fast however. Started acting different before she even spoke. "Holy shit! You filthy little Slut!" He exclaimed. TO ME! He was looking down with a look of horror on his face. "I only love your beautiful Sister and will not let you suck my cock ever you ugly worthless Whore!" He looked to my Sister with sorrow on his face and in his voice. "Thank God you came and saved me hunny! I was only trying to pee when she came in butt naked and tried to take me away from you Baby!" My nightshirt was laying on the floor and he was still holding my arm but it did not matter anymore.

Sis is not very bright! Violent? Yes! Crazy? Yes! Murderous? Apparently.

She just went total Ape shit! Not saying a thing. Saw the switch flipped in her head trough her eyes and knew I was done. Grabbing Mom's hair dryer from a shelf she just smashed it to pieces on my head with one hard, savage blow. It shattered she hit me so hard. Both my skull and the hair dryer! Her rage made her strength unbelievable. Pieces of plastic flew everywhere. Except those embedded in my head. Saw both darkness and bright light with the unbelievably intense pain I felt. They both proceeded to beat me so very bad on the toilet my blood was really everywhere. My Sister screaming unintelligibly at me the whole time. Then coldly I heard her say. "The only thing for a piece of SHIT like you is a plunger!" Father held me down for her with glee while she raped and beat me savagely with it over and over laughing manically until I passed out from the pain and blood loss after a while. That pain was so great remembering it hurts! She did some very big damage inside me down there! Doctors were amazed I survived but assured my Mother I would never have kids. Frankly I suspect I didn't survive. Pretty sure I died then for the first time. Woke in agony after a while to see them both in the shower doing it! Her legs wrapped around his waist as he bounced her on himself and she was laughing gleefully! She called him her Husband! He called her his Wife!

     Blackness took me again!

     The next thing I can remember for sure was waking in the hospital all alone. Could not move when I woke and it scared me. Arm was in a cast strapped to my chest. Leg was in one as well and hung up in traction. Strapped down on the bed! Only one eye opened yet and I cried at my vague memorys and savage pain. Finally a nurse came in and when she saw I was actually awake she freaked. Know how bad I looked when I left the hospital two weeks later so I know I was hideous then but that was not why she freaked. My face is not right anymore. Went from a not so pretty Girl to a misshapen one. Nothing grotesque. Just does not look right. The Doctors could only do so much they said! Our insurance sucked as well so any future cosmetic surgery was unthinkable. The internal damage was too much to ever work again they said. Would never have children they told me. Maybe why the dream of having Puppys was so wonderful. My Mom seemed more hurt by this than me. Well her dreams of Grandchildren were forever gone now. Had been in a coma for over five days and they had talked of pulling the plug as they thought I was brain dead! Ever drop an egg? My skull looked worse on the X-Rays. That I even woke completely amazed the Doctors! Their machines had detected no real brain function left in me for days. Had been dead too long.

     Found out later I had somehow, amazingly, with both a broken arm and leg, crawled out of the house it seems in an attempt to escape and the neighbors Dog found me naked and bleeding in the bushes between our houses in the wee hours of morning. Cops and EMT's came fast and finally by following my blood trail back through the open backdoor they found my Father and Sister passed out naked in bed together! My little Brother was babbling in a closet. My Sister attacked the Officers violently as they tried to understandably cuff our Father! Hurt two of them bad before they tasered her! Regret not seeing that. All nine times! About the only thing her and I ever had in common. We could take a lot of abuse! They finally cuffed her and tossed her in a Squad Car.

     My Sister was so pissed when she found out I was not dead however, screaming she wanted to kill me and should have slit my worthless throat, she kicked out a Cop car window to try and get me again. They don't think she will ever get out of the mental hospital. Hopefully not! Father took a plea deal for ten years. Eligible for parole in five. They killed him in there long before he got parole. Not sure how they got my address but the three Prisoners who killed him write me still. They had written me and told me what they did to him in there in graphic detail and it made me smile. Made his life hell before they ended it! Letters were found however and only my therapist kept those Men from getting in any trouble. She knew I felt so much better after I got a letter from one of them and convinced the courts to let them continue writing to me. Nicer to me than anyone else. Had mailed out their Christmas cards last week!

     Mom only got some probation and religion! Not sure why she got either one. Has a nice Church Man now. Well he treats her nice. Could not handle him either however. He always looked at me like my Mother's pain was my fault! Could be because I died and they revived me. Three times! They had no idea why I even lived. Found out I should not have lived eventually! Doctors were clueless. Frankly I am sure God could have found an easier way to get things to happen and I told Church Dude that. Many times. Yeah he was all, "God's Plan, God's Will," and shit! Hated Church as it was pure denial! Everything is God's will so no one has to take responsibility for their mistakes. Still I loved Christmas! Not so much Jesus! Christmas is not the Anniversary of his birth either! He was born in April! Says so in the Bible! The Norse festival of Yule was turned into Christmas by the Romans to appease the Pagans!

     Only way to control the Pagans! Corrupt them slowly! The way of religion.

     Okay! Now I needed to purge these thoughts from my head! This was going to be the best Christmas I ever had as it was gonna make it on my terms! And I was gonna be a Dog for it damn it! The Pack BITCH! The Alpha Female! Yes I snickered inside at that thought. Might have been crazy then! Hard to really know. No longer human but not yet Dog. Never asked to be human. Wanted to be a DOG!

     Pulling myself out of the Pile I nuzzled Fenrir awake and turning stood there wiggling my rump, offering myself to him. No! Demanding to be serviced! MY PACK! HE hesitated so I Woofed loud at him! Not quite sure what was going on he knew it was an offer and he was not going to pass it up. Whimpering as he mounted me I shifted myself to get him in there fast. My desire and need was all that mattered and I let him know. HE was growling deep in his throat quick but it was a happy sound! Well I was making some very happy sounds too! More Pig grunts but happy Pig grunts! Oh it was tremendous when you wanted it. Attitude does make a difference in most things but especially SEX! The more you get into it the greater the sensations become. Love the one you're with. Passionately!

Gave a bark and a loud sniff till someone understood and Cerberus put his butt in my face. Sniffed and licked his tooter passionately in joy! Maybe I truly had gone crazy. Could be brain damage! When I got out of the hospital they said to avoid ever hitting my head again or it may kill me! Told an old Boyfriend that once and when he got pissed at me he hit my head on everything he could find! Wanted me dead and told me so! Day after Day! No idea really but I knew I was happy at that moment sane or not and that is what truly counts. Tried very hard to keep him inside me this time! Clenching my pussy muscles tight! Oh the throbbing was good on the G spot. Managed to keep him in till after he made the tie at least. It was so cool being butt to butt with him even if for only a moment. Those big warm balls pressed against my butt cheek felt great. He came out though and rather fast.

Knew I needed to strengthen those muscles if I hoped to hold them in there. Knew how to get practice too and as soon as he was out I spun and shoved my tushy in Apollo's snout. My control! As he mounted me I saw Fenrir lay in front of me as he began to lick himself. Oh Bad Boy! That was mine to lick. Growling at him I pushed my head in there and thinking candy cane went nuts on it as Apollo hammered my backside like I was a Bitch in heat. Such rapid fire, jack hammer action! So intense I wanted to howl! Had a candy cane in my mouth though.

Was Christmas time.

Lost in my lust I guess as I did not even realize Apollo had made the tie. Held him for a while! Only a minute but it was awesome! Panted and whined my joy like a Bitch in heat! The happyness in the Boys at this behavior from me was very noticeable. Had no idea what they understood or how but they knew I was one of them now. That I had chosen them! Happy Dogs!

Cerberus was bigger then the other two. Both ways! Stuck my rump in his snout and whimpered my desire without hesitation. Oh, he licked me for a minute cleaning up his Pack mates cum first then he was up. Already delirious from multiple orgasms I was shaking beneath him. Yes drooling as well. Apollo saw it, it seems, and came around pushing his head under my chin and between my arms. Thought he was only going for the breasts but he kept going till he was under me. Supporting me a bit! Oh I sniffed at him and Fenrir came pushing his butt at my face too. Damn right I licked and not just his poophole either. Such a fascinating texture on Dog balls. Recommend them!

It was a strain on me however but I held Cerberus in me after the tie for five minutes. There was a clock in there. Had worried about boredom as a Dog but two hours of sex a couple times a day would eat up a lot of free time now! Had licked all of them after they came out of me. It was the least I could do! Liked the taste even I found. Subtle as well but I knew there was a difference between them. Thoughts came in my head. Strange thoughts! Pushed out by the hunger in my tummy.

In the kitchen I went to the cupboards and opened them with my snout and teeth very careful to not use my hands, till I found what I needed. MY own food dish! Interesting stuff in there but I was hungry so I dragged a bowl out onto the floor with my mouth. It was stoneware like the others but a pinkish color. MINE! Had my name on it even! Athena! Was my name mow! Tag said so! Mallory was dead! For the last time! Was now Athena! Pushed the cupboard door closed with my snout and pushed my dish over to the feeder the same way. Like the Dog I now was. Held my head high as I pushed the button on the floor with my palm and my dish filled. Pushed it out of the way and they proudly took turns filling theirs.

Sure I wondered why he needed a Dog sitter if they could feed themselves. Kinda understood however as if something happened no one would know or could help. Yes, I thought I was set up as well but realized quick there was no way he had any control in it. Right? Not all of it, that was certain. That he loved his Dogs was apparent. There were Dog's pictures everywhere here. Hmm. Idea! Had to look later and see if there were pictures of Athena anywhere. Boy this food was not that bad. Just took some getting used too I guessed. Hey I won't eat liver but Liverwurst is fine! Go figure that one! Besides I ate so fast by now I barely tasted it till I was done anyway. Water!

Never hesitated after drinking and headed straight for the Doggy door. It was not snowing outside anymore and the world looked so fresh and beautiful in a thick layer of white I hesitated for a moment. Well until a cold wet nose shoved me rather playfully from behind. Went out fast through the deep snow happily. Freezing certainly but it was so liberating and fun as snow flew around me as I raced through it. Naked and free! Sniffing around like one of them I found a smell so I went pee there! Seemed the right thing to do then. Ah piddle piddle! Had to go a bit I guess. Lots of yellow snow? Not exactly. Looked like a snow cone! Sniffed my own pee! Was curious. Smelled different then theirs. Red too though and I realized suddenly my period was a part of this. Thought they were just being nice licking me back there. Had forgotten all about it! Knew a Bitch bled when in heat however. Did they think I was in HEAT? Was that why they attacked me? Could they smell the blood and it excited them? Knew Bear were attracted to Women on their periods! Really seemed like it now that I thought about it. Still they were nice. Tasted my own pee. Not bad I guess. Oops. Sniffed around more. Seemed the right spot. Squat and Poop. Yes I sniffed it too. Did not smell good! Was I sick?

Cold already but I felt I really had to do it, so I went to where each had gone potty and sniffed and tasted. Both their pee and poop. Saw Cerberus eat my poop. Wanted to let them see and know I wanted to be one of them but could not do it! I could not... Lick! The taste was not pleasant but? No! Different for each one though I realized when I was done. Just like with the urine. Trotted back in the house. Weird thoughts went through my head then. Kind of Dog thoughts! Believe me I was messed up! It was so free being a Dog however! No schedules! No alarms! No one telling you what to do every minute of every day! No one hitting you or screaming at you. Just relax and play! Well I include fucking in the play part! Oh it was so much fun! We Played a lot!

Still unsure how far I would take it I found myself wondering how Professor Murphy would react to me when he came back and found me naked with them! Would he watch? Could always have sex with him if I had too! Worked with most guys after all. Yes I used sex to get things in my life. My body was the only thing I had going for me these days and that was not much sadly! Did not look pretty anymore after all! Walked funny even. The broken leg was shattered and now shorter as they did not get back together right. One eye was deeper then the other which made my face look funny. If I got on my knees and sucked a guy off he did not have to see my uglyness so I got very good at that. No idea how many times I wished I had died back then! Then again Insanity ran in the family it seems! At least on my Father's side. Maybe the Professor would see how much the Boys loved me and just keep me! Could stay a Dog forever if it meant being happy and safe! Being human fucking sucked!

Had almost two weeks still before he would come back so I need not worry about it now. So I could just play and have fun. Was getting that feeling inside me again however as it was getting dark outside. New sensation that one was! That desire for and craving of SEX! Chocolate or ice cream yes but sex? Never! Now I wanted it like I was a real BITCH in heat! An insatiable need! Wondered if it truly was madness I was experiencing? But it was very strong now and by God I was Happy here!

Went over to Apollo and shoved my snout under him and sniffed then licked at his furry cock sheath letting him know my interest well. He got the message quick however. Smart Boy! Around behind me he went and was up, on, and in me fast. Oh! Rough, fast, jack-hammer furry sex is beyond description! Trust me. Those furry legs wrapped around my waist like he would never let me go filled my heart with joy! Hoped he never did as I felt for once safe under him! All of them made me feel safe and loved. Kind of knew any or all of them would kill or die for me. Their loyalty and willingness beyond questioning as they were Dogs. MY Boys! All that said the fur tickled my butt and the back of my legs a lot. Was very ticklish there so I may have giggled like a crazy person while being stuffed with some big Dog-Cock! Very happy crazy person!

Clamped my muscles tight with determination on him down there as I felt him begin to swell inside me. My Dog-Cock now! Whimpered my tremendous lust and desire for him. It meant. "Fill me with your seed"! "Give me your Puppys!" At that moment I wanted it so bad, even if I knew it was impossible! Pretty sure I thought I could at that moment too. Like I said I was gone! Felt so amazingly free inside though! Something I never knew before! The extreme orgasms may have helped all that I guess. Oh they were extreme and I howled for each one. Unlike anything a human had ever given me. Well these were filled with pure love. Wanted something bad however! Tried to hold them in but it did not work. Not strong enough down there yet but wanted it more than anything. So when Cerberus went up last I hunched so he got the hole I needed him in. Drove that huge thing deep in my plump ass whimpering his joy! He really liked that hole too! Oh Baby! He was mine for the next half hour Damn it! My Stud! So now I was Cerberus's Bitch! I WAS ATHENA!

Made the tie and he was not coming out for a while. He was so swollen inside me I feared he may potentially rupture my colon but found I just did not care! Knew I would die for them. Snickering nastily I went to the kitchen to get a drink and some more food. Damn right I was dragging his big fluffy butt with me! Think he was laughing as he walked backwards! Still had some food in my dish. Had a two hundred pound butt plug buried deep in me and I loved it! He went with me gladly. His way of saying I was not his but he was mine? Giving himself to me? How sweet! True love!

Once loose it was out the Doggy door to pee one last time I went. Interesting thing is the fact that orgasms fill you with things called endorphins which are natures painkillers so pain and cold are not so noticeable.! Not necessarily a good thing though! Got kinda carried away a bit as I did not feel the cold much and tackled Fenrir from the side into the snow! Oh it was on. The other two joined in and we beat up Fenrir. Okay we just roughed him a bit. He let us do it to him. Knew I would make it up to him. It was his sharp bark that brought them to attention however. They all quickly forced me into the house before I even realized how very hard I was shivering. Went to Fenrir once inside and whimpering I rubbed on him to say thank you. Knew I was in bad shape now as I had trouble even moving once inside. Gently they pushed me all the way to the den where I collapsed in a Dog bed and they were on me and covering me in a moment. Oh, it was warm, trust me. Big fluffy Dogs. Not sure if he did it on purpose or not however Fenrir's butt was in my face. Buried my face in it and cleaned his tooterhole happily for him. It was right there and it probably itched I thought. Felt him sigh when I pushed my tongue in a little. You try not wiping and see how quick you're scratching there! Felt him fart too when he did and I just sniffed harder. For the first time in years, maybe ever I felt both loved and part of a family!

Trust me! My past life was HELL!

CHAPTER 3 ALPHA BITCH Friday December 21st

Drifted in and out of sleep for a while. Warm though. They were making sure of that. Maybe I was delirious as I felt strangely weird. Then again it may have been the Methane! Fenrir was a gassy Boy! Not a complaint you see. Yes I sniffed him and well, whenever I could. Smelled bad in a way but it had a scent of some kind in there that said friend! No I can not describe it. It is weird but realizing this made me finally start wondering if I was changing somehow? Did not feel right in so many ways! Had assumed it was just all from my beating by an Asshole still. But was it? Not bad feeling mind you, but only different. It's just that so much had changed in my physical perceptions already. Maybe it was only because I was half asleep and not thinking straight. Felt different no matter what. They say when a person loses their sight the other senses will improve to compensate. Maybe something like that was going on here. Could be brain damage! No idea. Hoped I was okay.

Woke completely finally and the whole world felt very different to me! Not in a bad way mind you. Sounds and smells were suddenly so much sharper it felt. Not necessarily a good thing with a gassy Dog butt in your face however. Not a bad smell anymore but very strong! Certain it smelled like all the others had it just did not bother me like before. Curious? Woke him up! Yes I put my tongue up his butt. He Woofed happily at that. My butt was really sore. Oh not the butt hole! Up higher. Just a strong ache. Wondered if all that humping bruised my tail bone.

Bled during the night however and someone was licking my ass clean. Smelled the blood so I knew. It was a strong smell as well but I felt little. Was my sense of smell stronger? They got up off of me and we headed right for the kitchen where I went straight for the Doggy door and out into the snow without a second thought. So bright out there this morning. The sun was peaking through the low hanging clouds and the whole world looked so bright and new too me!

Through the drifts I pushed with utter joy now. Once out what seemed far enough I began sniffing around. Ahh, this was a good spot! Squat and pee! Looked at the others. They were peeing as well. Crawl around sniffing. Hunch my back and poop! Ah that felt good. Wished I had toilet paper. My butthole itched! Was extremely hungry, and I mean ravenous, but I still went to where one of the Boys had peed. Knew it was fresh right away! Could smell that fact. Strange but I liked this aspect of things. So amazing to know what was fresh.

Head down I sniffed and licked. Taste! Oh amazing flavor! Did not taste like I expected. Was kind of nice really. Went to find more. Again, sniff and lick. Ooh, smelled something else. One had pooped over here! Had to find it. Went and sniffed at it fast. Cerberus it smelled like! Head down to sniff again to be sure.

Swallowed before I even realized what I had just done! Part of the poop was missing! With a bite taken out of it! BY ME! With horror in my eyes and head, I bent again and took another bite! A part of me was appalled.

Head up I thought. "That was good!" And trotted to the house with poop breath! Fenrir went and ate mine! He had poop breath too the naughty Boy! Brain lock maybe I thought. Filled my dish and ate Dog Food greedily. Tasted great after Poop! Poop tasted rather good as well. The Pack watched me eat closely for some reason. Thought maybe they were just afraid I was cold again so I shrugged it off. Once we all had eaten I went exploring a bit. They happily followed. Had been here two days and had seen nothing of the house. Motion sensors turned the lights on for us in most areas as we went. The dim lights in the Den stayed on always. So did the kitchen. Front hall was still on as I had never turned them off! Now I looked up at them and Apollo barked. Ooh they went out. Bark On, Bark Off technology! This house was really very high tech. Especially for a Dog! No way in hell he could afford this house on a Teacher's salary.

Could probably snoop around some and find things out but it did not matter really. My Home! Would not have helped me if I did find anything any way. Trust me! Found a big bathroom on the ground floor though! Just by the Den! Figured there had to be one around down here and now I had found it. Cerberus quickly took advantage of the open toilet seat and got himself a nice drink. Snickered at him. Went next?! A vague horror filled me but did not stop me from going and lapping toilet water. Out of the bowl! There was a sort of large glass door shower stall in there as well. It was really big! Looked closer and saw it held a few Dog shampoos. Yep! Big enough to wash Moose in I thought!

Went further in the house on hands and knees. Every room was very nice to the point I assumed the Professor had to be gay! Or else he had a gay interior decorator! No straight guy could make a home this beautiful! Sorry straight guys, there are some things you just can't do! Interior decorating and taking a dick up the ass both come to mind! Some things you straight guys can do exceptionally well. Maybe he was Martha Stewart's nephew! This place was quite practical but put anything in Better Homes and Gardens to shame! Then we got to the livingroom! Oh WOW! It was a storybook room with a twenty foot tall perfectly decorated Yule tree in it. Well it had twenty foot high ceilings! Barely noticed anything else for a minute it was so beautiful. Big, grand stone fireplace at one end with a real bearskin rug in front of it. Gorgeously wrapped presents were already under the tree. GAY! No straight Man could wrap that beautifully. Rapidly I went over and looked. Many were for the Moose I mean Dogs! Like gay people. Several of the packages had Female names. Two were repeated and a lot. Laura and Becky. Wondered who they were. A few had no names that I saw. Some had the Dogs names on them.

Barking on a hunch the tree lit up so brilliant for me. Not what I wanted now was it. Wiggle wiggle! Fenrir mounted me quick knowing full well what I wanted. Both of us were just panting fast as he hammered hard swelling Dog-Cock into me practically under the glorious tree. Such ecstasy in me! Yes his Cock was Ecstasy! Beyond anything I ever had in my life! Because of what my Sister did to me I never got much pleasure before either. Physically and emotionally I was in paradise! The other two came up to us and rubbed on me as Fenrir slipped off and pulled his one leg over my ass till he made the tie. The strong sensations down there inside me felt different I suddenly realized. More intense sure, but not the same either. Kinda better! Felt my muscles clamping down on their own. hard, on his throbbing cock. Felt every throb of that amazing tool too as it pumped it's hot gooey Doggy cum in me so well.

My whole pussy throbbed in time with it sending waves of pleasure through me! Nervous I took a step forward. He backed up as I pulled him! No idea how or why, but he was not coming out of me for a while at least and I could feel that. My vaginal muscles were clenched so tight around his penis now I felt sending waves of sensation through me. So amazing! Howled my joy than! Was a good howl too. Sounded real. They got excited at that! Somehow they knew what my joy was! Two hours of almost constant throbbing Dog-Cock locked in me one after the other! Oh my I was so damn happy. Drooled a lot however! Cerberus Drooled a lot as well! The other two not so much. All had gas however. Well I did too and every fart I let, a snout got shoved into my butt. So nice. They liked me smelling theirs as well. Could tell as they would now stick it in my face before farting! Naughty Boys! Kissed them for the gift. With tongue.

Gave me time to think just standing there on all fours. Not sure that was a good thing! Was acting a lot like a Dog now wasn't I? Drinking from the toilet! Eating yellow snow! Eating Dog Poop! Seriously not normal human behavior! Pretty normal for Dogs though! Okay a part of me was repulsed still but it was not in charge any more and it had lost all control and was growing smaller. My inner Dog was in the drivers seat! Did not bother me. Yeah I thought about how nice it would be to have a litter of Pups by my Boys. No idea how long I had been thinking that dreamily before I realized it but it was a while!

Yes I wanted it! Knew it was totally impossible though. How much impossible stuff do you want? Maybe! Was Christmas.

Tired after getting fucked so well by all three I went to the Den and they all lay with me. Stuffed my snout in Apollo's tushy and slept. My whole body ached when I woke. Not bad pain mind you, just a dull ache like I had a really intense workout yesterday. But they did all the work! Just kind of stood there myself. Got up and stretched! That felt pretty weird as well. Cool however. Trotted to the bathroom and drank from the toilet again. It was closer then the water dish in the kitchen. Yeah only thirty feet or so but hey it's thirty feet and I was thirsty. Maybe that was why the lid and seat were up. He loved these Dogs immensely I could tell. They were treated like Family! Like don't you make your relatives drink out of the toilet? Knew I loved these Dogs! Realization set in now. So I did. Not just Owner-Pet type love either. Wanted to mate with them forever! Ran from one Boyfriend that abused me only to end up with three that loved me back! Not bad huh?

Was like, Wow! Took a moment and examined the feelings inside me and knew fast I had never felt this way before. About anything! Went outside to potty. Sure I was going right past my water dish! Haven't you ever been so thirsty you could not wait to make the kitchen? Know some of you have tasted toilet water. Do not deny it! We know some of you swallowed during your swirlys too! Smelled something completely different the moment I was out the door. Sniffing the air I went toward the back fence. It was a very tall wire mesh hurricane fence. Looked like it had Razor Wire on top. Odd. Something had been out there in the snow however. Could not be sure without standing but I quickly suspected Deer tracks would be found. So that was how a Deer smelled! No I didn't stand. Why would I want too? Snow was deep out here by the fence. Head barely over it as I pushed my chest through a drift.

"WOOF!" Fenrir barked sharply! Now I was never an athletic person before. Still I now managed to leap and spin sending snow flying as I barked back at him. He got excited and plowed his way to me and I ducked under the snow. When he got close I pounced. He moved fast and POOF! Snow flew! Powder snow is fun for Dogs. To add insult to injury however he lifted his leg on me quickly. Yes I lay naked in the snow waiting for him to finish pissing on me. Rolled in the snow when he was done before getting up and peeing myself. Head for the house! Wearing Dog pee. You need to be a Dog too understand.

Such freedom and joy in being a Dog! Not feeling very cold in spite of what I had just done I sat on my butt in the kitchen and licked what pee I could reach off me. Liked the taste or I would have just left it all!

Played more Doggy games. Had fun racing through the house. Went outside again! Did not hesitate to eat Apollo's poop this time! My humanity was slipping away rapidly and I knew it! Did not care however and had no idea why. Was only wondering if the Professor would keep me when he got back. Hoped so!

The pain in my rump was finally gone at least! As well as the belly cramping! Hands and legs ached now however. Figured that was just from crawling so much so I thought nothing of it.

Got frisky and as Cerberus mounted me I felt something back there shift.

Before I could think about what I felt I felt something else shoving in me as I was being plowed hard! That will distract you! Felt different as well but so much more amazing. My heart was so full of love for these Brut's I feared it would burst. By the time they were done I was pretty much fucked senseless however! Oh I was! Wobbly so I sat on my rump. OWW! Had I sat on something? Got up and looked. Nothing there. Big mirror in the bathroom?! Went there to look at what hurt.

Um this may be a bit of a problem I thought! Well I had a fluffy tail! Maybe only six inches long but a real TAIL! Ooh my butt was cute with it. Always had a nice butt. So I practiced wagging my tail. So adorable! Took some practice before I got the hang of it too. Wondered how long it had been there. Remembered the ache back there in that spot and thought not long. Liked it sure, but why did I have it? The real problem however would only come when I had to leave. Planned on begging to stay if I had too. Do anything to stay here now!

Still I better go show it off and wag it nice for the Boys I thought! Yes I was happy! Eat again. Now show it off! Went and wiggled and wagged for them. They seemed to truly love it! Taught me how to chase my own tail now. There seems to be an actual reason to it. No idea what though. Still fun! So very excited however with my new found Doggyness! Wanted to learn all the Doggy secrets now!

Knew this may be all in my head. Crazy or dying? Hoped not!

Laying there being cozy Fenrir perked up looking toward the front of the house. We watched! All of us were attentive! Then I thought I heard something. We listened for a while. None of the Dogs got up to go look! Then I remembered the motion sensors for the lights. Not sure the Boys understood that I wondered.

If someone were outside and lights came on they would probably run. Probably! If we waited and they came in we could surprise them however. Bite them and pee on them! Had a problem though.

Waited as long as I could before getting up, then headed for the kitchen. Went outside cautiously sniffing and aware of the scents. Caught a smell fast. It was weak but I knew my nose was probably nowhere near as good as a real Dog yet. It was a familiar scent though. Then I placed it! SWEAT! Humans had been out here in the woods somewhere. Went sharp left, hugging the house till I got to the fence. Sniffing hard I went up on my hind feet and…. HIND FEET? Cool I had hind feet! Okay paws now! Well I always had short legs but this was just OH MY! When had this happened to me? Still kinda human legs but very short. Had paid no attention to it. Totally unaware I had not been on my knees all this time. Not sure when I had last.

Had to focus now. Looked out there for signs of intruders. Nothing! Follow the fence and up again. Went the whole way around going up every ten feet but could see nothing. Squatted and peed. Sniff it! Sniff around. Ahh! Squat and poop! Apollo came out and looking around as I had he to finally went potty. Sniffed and licked his pee and poop. Well it was fun! And tasty! Also made the bond between us something more! Just kinda knew some how! Maybe that was what made us scent stronger marking us as friends?

In I went and to the bathroom quick where I checked myself out. Tail was much longer now! Legs shorter by a bit! Body looked longer but I could not tell for sure. Looking cool however. All definite improvements to me though I thought. Becoming a Dog for Christmas! Best present I ever got by far!

To the kitchen. They had my dish full for me already. They loved me and I rubbed my thanks on them and ate heartily. Kinda good stuff really. Once done they checked me out just sniffing everything. Seemed to approve of the new me. Maybe too much? Barely made it to the Den before being mounted by one of them roughly! (Rape me Boys! I am yours!)

Felt very different this time. Lots better however! Hard too think much while they made me their Bitch once again. Wanted it so bad too! Who needed to think? All three of them one after the other pushing those huge throbbing things in me, driving me to the heights of Ecstasy wiped me out in the most amazing way! Barely made a bed.

Thought more as I lay there. My body was changing a lot! Something had been done to me somehow! Could not do this on my own I was certain! The question was how? Had to be some king of drug! All I had eaten besides Dog food here was poop after all! My mind seemed okay so I did not think it was in the Dog food. If it were it would effect the Boys as well and that I felt he would not do. Then it hit me! When I met the Professor it was at the cafe. And I had gone to the bathroom right away! Leaving him alone with my drink! Had he somehow gone and slipped something in my drink? But what? Some kind of mutational drug! Had to be something amazing to do this I knew. My body was changing after all.

Last thought I remember having was I should thank him.

CHAPTER 4 FAMILY'S Saturday December 22nd

Jumped up fast and I was quickly barking my head off in a panic at the horrible loud sound that suddenly rang throughout the house! Boys did as well but they quickly settled down as I kept freaking. Sure it seemed a kind of familiar loud horrible noise and the Boys seemed to understand it. Almost too loud it seemed to me. Recognized it myself suddenly now and stopped freaking. SNOW PLOW! It was still dark out. Winter Solstice! Was the shortest day of the year so it meant little. Clock said only seven ten. Still early! Would not be light for an hour! Doesn't he know Dogs are sleeping? Not too early for a plow truck it seems! Thought to myself. "I should call him! Wait! I didn't call him!" Well the Professor said I would have to, right? Should have figured out something but I was overwhelmed by my new senses. Knew that truck sounded very loud to me! Much louder than it would have to Mallory. Had my hearing improved that much?

Padded out of the room making my way to the front of the house to see and understand. My Pack followed my tail. Livingroom! Looking out the big picture window behind the couch. There was a rather beat up pick up truck with a large plow on it out there scraping the huge driveway around my car! Loud! Louder than it should have been! This was amazing! Hearing was greatly improved! The Man driving tooted and waved at us quick. Was impressed he saw us in the window. Had quite a bit of experience with the plow the way he went around my car too. Probably with the house as well. Explained why the Dogs did not freak. They knew this truck and it's sound! Still I didn't call him. Maybe he thought the Professor was still here and just came? Okay I was pretty sure I was in many ways a Dog now and I had freaked. Did not feel human anymore in the least. My mind was still here but the rest was going pure Dog and fast it seemed. We watched him work curious. He left with another toot and a wave. Friendly guy.

Speaking of toots we all were as well and the livingroom now stunk! Head for the back door. Out and do our "Business". Sure I went around and sniffed them all when they were done. Ate some but you knew that. It's a Dog thing! Really it is! They learn so much from it. So I was looking down my nose at a Cerberus poop pile when it hit me! Well I was actually looking down my nose! Well snout, because I had one now! Nose was a dark pink but definitely Canine! Looked so cute! No fur there yet. Pretty sure my butt was furry now though. Eat more poop quick and head in. Straight to the bathroom and those big Mirrors. Yep! Furry butt! COOL! Tail was so long and hairy now as well. Nice red fur! Must be an Irish Setter! Wagged it all sexy like. Not sure of the floppy lips I now had but I liked the floppy ears. Very cute! Extra Long tongue! Hung out nicely when I panted. Flexible too. Picked my own nose with it just to see if I could. Ooh! Tickled! Well I was now interesting looking to say the least. Really cool I thought! Did not look like either human or Dog at the moment, but a lot of both were visible. This was just astounding! Would lick the Professor my thanks when he came home! Certainly could not suck him with my new mouth. What amazing Canine teeth I had.

Go eat! Food this time. Poop is really good but only so much of it out there and I was hungry! Good stuff! Definitely a Dog thing but let us face it!

I was now a Dog! For better or worse! I think for Better!

We all heard the front door opening as we ate. Interesting? Had not heard a car! Maybe it was robbers? The Boys ran to see who was here all excited like. Maybe too happy! Wondered if it were robbers would the Boys just follow them around hoping for treats? Remembered how that went for me however so I went fast after them just in case I had to save someone from being sat on! Unless they deserved it! They had all stopped short! Looking extremely nervous! Not who they expected to see but someone they knew! So I looked. A tall, elegant, gorgeous, blonde Woman in an expensive suit dress and winter coat stood there glaring at the Dogs! Yikes!

Then she saw me! Eyes went wide for only a second. "Oh great!" She exclaimed loudly sounding disgusted looking at me as I came in. Oh I knew that voice could be so much nastier if she wanted it to be so I just kinda panted looking back trying my best too look kinda friendly like.

A gentler adorably sweet voice from outside asked sounding sort of worried. "What is it Mom?"

The Lady suddenly smiled wickedly saying. "Your Father got another Dog!" Then a bit quieter, voice softer. Perhaps too me. "Very pretty Girl too." It was true! Yes I was now very pretty! The damage to my face that had been there for so long was just gone. Had seen that right away. That she saw and just accepted me as a Dog should have told me something.

Did not try to talk! Well I Knew she would not be able to understand me if I tried. Floppy Dog lips you see! You try talking without using your lips! However there was no screaming from her so I thought it was okay for the moment. Hey I was obviously not a Dog but she knew something and accepted me. Well she had keys in her hand and acted like she belonged here and hey there was my purse! On the sideboard! Knew then I had already smelled traces of her here! Very faint but she knew the Professor and my Boys! She smelled really nice as well. Had her phone out now looking quickly at something on it intently and ignoring us. A bit shorter, bit cuter, bit pudgier, strawberry blonde, Girl, with her arms full of bags pushed in behind her Mother now shutting the door behind her with a foot. Spotting me however she instantly dropped her bags and with her mouth hanging open she went to her knees arms spread wide. All four of us went to her happily.

She smelled so nice. She hugged us all so well too. Yes even me! Looked kinda like a Dog sure but unless she was totally blind she knew full well I was part human. Still she hugged me also! Very squishy Girl. Liked her right away. That is the way of the Dog! Friend or foe in a second.

The Woman had been watching me closely but her phone as well. The Girl who was probably my age, maybe a year younger, finally got my head up and looked at my tag. She gasped loud now. "He named her Athena?!" Her voice held what? Horror? Anger? Sadness? All three?

Her Mother laughed gently at that shaking her head. "Oh I don't think your Father named her dear. From what I just saw the Boys actually gave her the collar." Must have gotten a shocked look on my face at this! This Woman smiled gently down at me now and her voice held such laughter. "Yes Girl. The whole house is watched. Cameras pretty much everywhere. Likes to check in and see how the Boys are when he is at work. To make sure you are nice to his Baby's as well you understand. From what I saw however you have been? Well? Very accommodating to the Boys. Maybe too much? Can you speak?" WOOF! Kind of embarrassed completely too but hey? "No Girl. I mean talk. Like a human." Just shrugged. It was a maybe at best. "Alright! Yeah I kinda understand Girl. It's okay. Floppy lips I get it! One question though and it's very important so be honest! Do you like being a Dog?" Her voice sounded very nervous yet curious now really. Some amazement was there but not as much as I would think. Took a second then nodded well knowing I did. Her voice was a little more strained now. Maybe even scared a bit. Cerberus had gone up to her and she was petting him nicely. "Well I can probably find out what he did to you and even why I am sure. Reversing it may be impossible however. You might have to be a Dog forever!" Not a problem for me. Much nicer to be a Dog than a human. WOOF! Yep I sniffed at her like the Dog I was becoming. Yep in her crotch! She did not stop me till my nose was in her butt. She scolded me then. "NO! Bad Girl! No sniffing Mama's butt!" Ooh! Now I really wanted it! Hey I had a Mama! Her voice was kinda shocked yet playful still. Turned to her Daughter and Mom spoke. "Let's get the rest of our stuff out of the car and in the house while we still have our coats on."

They went out and we Dogs followed! Yeah! Got to go outside! Sniffed around out here so very curious until I was suddenly attacked! Ooh sneak attack! Cerberus is a very big boy and he sent me deep into the soft snow on the side of the driveway. That was how he wanted it huh? Waited while he sniffed the snow I was buried in then pounced out sending him scurrying for safety. We played fast and furryous. Yes it is a word! Just wrote it, so now it is! Bite it! Or I'll bite you!

A sharp whistle finally got our attention. The pudgy Girl stood there holding the front door open happily waving us all in. She seemed so happy! We went. She touched me a bit as I went in. Ran her hand down my back. Ooh! Lots of luggage! Were they staying? Some wrapped packages too! Had played for a while it seemed as they had lots brought in. The very cute Pudge Butt headed to the Den and we Dogs followed. Her Mother was already sitting at the big desk with the computer and it's three monitors all on. She was watching ME on the monitors. My arrival and raping! Was a raping! Looked like I really enjoyed it though. Thought I did. The expressions on my face were so orgasmic! Also on the computer were documents of some kind she was cycling through fast enough I could not tell what they were. Faster then I could have done it. Then again she kind of knew what she looking for.

There was a large screen TV in here and the Girl sat all comfy like lounging on the big couch and turned it on. News channel! Was watching them both until I heard the announcer say. "The search for survivors of doomed flight 307 to Greece that was shot down by a Separatist Rebel missiles two days ago continues with little hope." WAIT! That was where the Professor was going. Was that his plane?

The cute pudge said from the couch sounding kinda sad answering my unspoken question. "Do you think Daddy survived Mom?!"

Mom just scoffed. "If he even made the flight which is unlikely knowing him, I'd say probably. You know how hard it is to kill your Father. Not like it was the first time they tried. What I want to know is how he did this. It is amazing!" She was pointing at me! "Well I can't find anything on here that would do this. Mostly only about his foolish healing bots. Seems like he actually got them working. And a while ago." Her voice held subtle contempt. She pointed at me again, patted her leg and said. "Come here Athena Girl!" Yep, it was my name now so I went when called. Liked the name a lot! She lifted my chin and looked intently in my eyes. "Did you perhaps eat or drink anything other then out of the Dog dishes?" Had to think. Crap! Well I had eaten that hadn't I? Nodded meekly. "What was it?" Nudged at her butt. Well hip. She started to get up and I shoved my nose in her butt! She gasped as she looked down at me her eyes wide in astonished horror and disbelief on the verge of laughter. "You actually drank from the toilet?" Nodded my shame. "Oh God! That's gross! No kisses from you! Anything else?" Snout in the butt again. She had not sat back down yet so I could. Took a moment till her eyes went even wider. "Oh that's grosser! Remind me never to kiss you!" She sat again and quickly. My thinking was if she kissed Dogs she could not be that bad of a person! Also thinking I wanted to kiss her! "Anything else?" Shook my head. Oh wait! Comprehending now I knew what she wanted. No, needed to know!

Finally realizing what she was after here I pushed her chair with her on it gently away from the computer with my head. Fingers were very short and I had

Canine claws but usable still I thought. New text document and I typed out my suspicions as she watched over my shoulder totally amazed by both me and my words, petting me like the I was Dog now as I typed what I suspected about the cafe! Could prove nothing yet.

Her voice was so loud right next to my ear and I knew she was speaking softly still. Her voice sounded good to me! This heightened hearing would take getting used too however. Time to adjust to my new senses! "That would explain some things Girl. At least how he got it in you, whatever it is? Just like him too! Never asks before he does stuff. Like a big child! If he comes back I may just put him in Diapers again!" The Pudge on the couch snort giggled. Then gentler and more concerned. "Why did you have to escape Girl? Tell Mama everything now. Take your time. Can't help you if I don't know." Looked at her sadly and she just nodded and hugged me tightly. So I had an owner now! Her word as owner was law so I typed no matter how much it hurt. She scratched behind my ear so nicely as I did what was asked. That is so nice! Heard more then one sob escape her lips as she read while I typed. By the time I was done the younger Girl had come over to read as well. Drawn by her Mothers tears? Both were in tears by the time I was done telling my horror. So I may have been as well. Both hugged me so tightly. "You will always be treated well here Girl!" Sounded good to me! Seemed like they wanted to keep me. Wanted to stay! Was home now.

Had to know for sure though so I typed one more thing. "I can stay?" Both said "Yes" together emphatically hugging me. So happily! The Mom Lady saved what I had typed. "We love our pets here Athena. You are family now! Do you mind being a pet?" Rubbed my head on her to get scratched as an answer. Sure as Hell Beat dying!

The three big Babys I mean Moose, (Moose Babys?) I mean Males had laid down in their beds being lazy. The Lady paused everything and said loudly. "Who wants to go for a walk?" Those lazy Boys were not lazy any more! One of the cool things about being a Dog! Sleep to wide awake in a flash! Worked the other way around as well! Waited at the front door patiently for the humans for what seemed an eternity. Time is different for us Dogs! Finally coats and hats and scarves and mittens on they opened a drawer in the buffet by the door and pulled out leashes! Four of them! "You choose first Becky." Ah so the Daughter was the mysterious Becky presents were for under the tree. Was the Mom Laura than? Most likely. Becky took me and Apollo. The two smallest Dogs! Made sense. Out we went and the big Boys behaved nicely. Long leashes though. Those Boys had some really big bladders too. Peed every ten feet I think. Where did they keep it all? Sniffed them all so I knew exactly how close they were. You thought I wouldn't?

Mom and the big Boys were in front of us when Fenrir stopped to poop and not thinking just reacting I sniffed it. YES! Ate it too! Becky snickered. "Nasty Girl!" We went all the way out to the road. About six hundred pee spots I sniffed along the way! Turned around and headed back. Us Dogs, our leashes long, at least twelve feet were having fun with the snow plowed up high on the sides of the driveway running up and down it and sinking in. Long leashes you see. Well I was on the top of a snow pile when I suddenly smelled it again. Becky squealed as I yanked the leash from her hand and headed off into the woods rather single minded. Knew that smell and they did not belong her!

Found the tracks in the snow easy. On a trail of sorts but they had stood around for a while! Sniffed them good too so I would remember who had been here! Yes so I could bite them if I ever found them! Nearest living neighbor was probably ten miles away. Becky caught up to me huffing and puffing in the deep powder. She instantly looked at the tracks too. Very intently as well, like she knew something. Her face looked very concerned by what she saw but she was praising me for being a good Girl. You could just see the house through the trees from here I noticed. They had been spying on us! Gonna BITE someone!

Went back together walking nicely beside her and Becky looked grim as we got close to the house. Knew those tracks were bad news. To her Mother she spoke once back! Sounded like a soldier giving a report I thought. "Three men were out there. Combat boots! Twenty cigarette butts!" She looked nervous too. Ooh I had not thought to count them! Had been out there a while now hadn't they? If they all smoked that was six a piece. Becky had a good eye for details as well as brains and an adorable pudge butt. Exactly how I liked my Chew Toys! Oh I was gonna chew on her! You just wait! "Stayed out behind the security perimeter too! Must know it's there!" Security perimeter? Getting more interesting nos but sounding even more dangerous!

Laura smiled wickedly now. "Well of course they knew it was there hunny. They also have no proof your Father was on that plane either. Might be why the search for bodies is so frantic! They have to know what happens if they access the house as well! Knew your Father would not leave it here too! Either they knew your Father did not have it on him or whoever shot it down wants to make sure it is destroyed. Without a body most of them will not believe he's dead either. They know your Father too well. He has us deep in it again!"

They talked as we walked. Becky was sounding nervous now. "Why would they want it destroyed? What was it Daddy was working on exactly anyway?"

The Mother, Laura, thought a moment before answering. You could see her wondering what to tell or maybe just how. "Best I can tell so far hunny is some how his bots had very strong healing ability's and could heal most things. Now that fact alone could prompt some major Pharmaceutical conglomerates to want it and him gone! His notes said it could heal practically anything!" She sounded very nervous about this for some reason. My mind however was racing.

Becky looked at her Mother. The look on her face was so confused as she made the leap I had not yet. "If it only heals damage why would it do this to Athena than?" A hitch was in her voice as she said my new name. Knew I was missing something here yet.

Laura's voice was quite gentle and Motherly sounding now. Like she was trying to teach her Daughter something. "Not really sure hunny. It might actually have a lot to do with her though. Well I just assume she got the Healing Nanos as your Father was apparently obsessed over them! Your Father is probably still putting those Dog growth hormones in the Boys food after all. Maybe other stuff too. Canine DNA could be a factor. The food and the semen combined." Her voice was rather gentle as she said all this. Like a Teacher explaining something to a student. Still I did not catch it.

Becky did and looked at ME shocked fast. "So they mated with her as well? She let them breed her?"

Hung my head in shame! Sounded like I was a Slut when you put it like that!

Laura rolled her eyes at this. Not the conversation you want to have with your Daughter! EVER! "Yes hunny. In the vagina probably had no effect but up the butt is a different story all together as the colon absorbs things and canine DNA would have been found by the Nanos. Best guess for now." Only a guess and it was wrong but she did not have all the facts yet. None of us did and yet the truth was there all the time staring us in the face.

Becky grabbed my snout gently but quick and turned me to look at her. In a shocked tone she asked. "You let those Boys hump your tushy?" Nodded well and I felt so ashamed. "Oh you kinky Bitch!" That last was said kinda playful. Her Mom just snickered. Nodded more timidly. Rubbing my head she said. "Good Girl!" She was not fooling me with her mock outrage. You see I could smell her excitement! Did she want to watch? Very nice scent!

So could the Boys it seemed. Still I wondered who was interested in what was in me rather then what they could put in me. So I was actually not thinking much about the Boys for a moment. Did not mind what was happening after all but I was curious none the less I found. What? Why? How? Us Dogs want to understand. Well would I soon be a full Dog? That may be a problem I felt. Was thinking like a Dog a lot. Not even hesitating before eating yellow snow or poop. Realized now how different my perceptions and thinking were! Still me in there but for how long? Would the Dog take over?

In the house they took coats and boots off. Forever it seemed to take! See what I mean? My perception of time was way off. Such a bother that clothing stuff was. Poor humans! Laura headed for the Den with the Boys following. They were sniffing at her! Boys! Becky said she would be right there as she had to go potty and I followed her. No idea why I followed her. Curious as to which potty she would use maybe? Might just be thirsty! The one down here was what she chose! Seeing me trialing behind her when she was about to shut the door she held it open for me with a sweet shy smile. She treated me like I was a real Dog and I was sure she wanted me to be. Not sure what she was thinking by doing this however. Or what I was thinking following for that matter. Went in and just sat on my haunches. That is my butt for you silly ignorant Humans! Very comfortable with a Dogs body. Kind of had one now.

She scratched my head going by but it kinda seemed she was pulling me along as she went over to the toilet so I scooted closer. Pulling down her thick snow pants and cute pantys she sat down on the toilet as I just watched. Got a glimpse of something furry in there! Squirrel? Could chase it for her if it was a Squirrel! She was cute down there I saw! Cute everywhere! Saw that bare pudge butt in the mirror as well! Began to drool for some reason. Adorable pudge everywhere! Scooted over even more rather nervously and just put my head in her lap as she began peeing! Trying to be friendly! I think? Could smell hot pee very well and her too for that matter! This new sense of smell was so totally awesome! My stupid abusive Boyfriend made me have a threesome one night with another Girl. She had been very nice! Really cute too! He of course had not been nice. To me or her! Maybe he thought we were enjoying each other too much and not him so he beat the hell out of both of us. He was right however! We were enjoying each other more. So very nice! Never saw her again. Made me sad.

Anyway, I could smell Becky! It was…? Very nice! "You are a weird one Athena." She looked down at me very thoughtful. "Do you really like the name Athena?" WOOFED! It was a great name for me! Felt so right! She giggled holding my head there as she began straining. Hmm. Was she? Ooh what an interesting smell hit me. Her poop smelled much nicer than the Boys did! Kinda like tacos! Of course she had a more interesting diet after all! She noticed my behavior however. Was sniffing pretty hard. Drooling in her lap as well so she asked coyly. "You like my poopy stink Athena?" WOOF! Smiling she spread her legs a bit. "Well get your snout in there and enjoy yourself Girl!" Very accommodating pudge Chew Toy I had here! Spreading her legs a bit more as I shifted around to be in front of her she actually pushed my head down there giving me a good look and smell. Such a cute Squirrel! How does it taste? Oh how I sniffed down there! Nervous as all hell let me say but I took a lick of her Girlhood. She yelped and jumped like she had not expected that, however she did not let my head up so I knew she was not upset. Held it down there even! The big thing about being a Dog is you need to smell and taste absolutely everything! Like an actual compulsion more than an obsession! Licked her more. Yep! This Squirrel still tasted great! Another thing about being a Dog is total lack of control. Yes I admit it! Knew full well shoving your head in a Girls crotch and licking her cervix was inappropriate for a Dog to say the least. Well I knew!

Still did not stop me. Tried so very hard to keep from losing all control here. Becky? Maybe not so much! Clawing at my head, which felt great, she soon moaned well. Did not help me control myself any! Seemed a lot like encouragement to me! A metallic voice full of laughter came from nowhere. "Really Becky? Sex with the new Dog? I'm shocked!" Liar Mommy! Did not sound like it to me!

Becky looked up. Did not see it you understand but I felt it. My head was still in the toilet and it was kinda dark. My tongue went in a redheaded Pudge's pooter. And I mean in! "Yes, gasp, Mother! Gasp. If I find a camera, gasp, In my, gasp, bathroom, gasp Dad better be dead! OH GOD!" She got loud as she came on my tongue already! Dog tongues are Damn amazing. Leaning forward on me a bit as I stopped she whispered panting and praising me. "GOOD GIRL! Did you like that? I sure did!" WOOF! Oops! She jumped at that. Had just barked in her crotch! Shame on me! Her Mom snickered! Pulled out of her. She sighed as she reached for the toilet paper and I just whimpered at her. Not by conscious choice but I was definitely not against it anymore. Really sorta wanted it now! Had smelled so yummy! Well I like Tacos! She looked at me shocked and cocked her head. Her voice held amazement. "Really girl?" No hesitation here I nodded good. "Gently please. That was a lot before." Standing slowly giving me a nice view of that Red Squirrel again. Such a cute Squirrel she had! Smiling she turned around and bent over the toilet and reached back spreading her adorable chubby cheeks. Such a cute butt this Pudge had as well. Had enough control now so I was gentle. Nice flavor too. Definitely Tacos last night. Would like more!

The snickering metallic voice came again sounding rather disgusted. "You're gross Becky!"

Snickering Becky replied breathless. "Don't knock it till you try it Mom! Damn amazing!" The joy in her voice was wonderful sounding and sent a thrill through me. Yes I had enjoyed it immensely. Wanted more! Sounded like she did as well! What joy! Gonna get me more Squirrel. Straightening up she lifted the seat instead of flushing! Huh? Looking at me very naughty like she said erotically. "Thirsty Girl?" Why YES I was! In that toilet so fast I slid. Bobbing for Becky Poopys! Yummy! "Get it all girl. Don't waste it." She had gone behind me as I feasted.

"Wow, that's so cool." Then a bit louder. "Can you see that Mom? She is definitely in heat!" She grabbed my puffy pussy. That felt real nice. "That is one puffy Bitch in Heat pussy!" Ooh! Really? Have to look when I'm done. Busy with my snack now!

The voice again. Laughter in it now. Possibly hysterical. "Are you examining her Becky or just repaying the favor?"

Becky snickered not answering. "Think she will be able to actually have Puppys? I really hope so." Damn right I woofed. Wanted them too! You can not begin to understand how I felt. Being a Dog is so wonderful! For me it was so much more. Most of my life I had been treated like a pile of shit. Here I was for once in my life treated nice and HAPPY! Loved more than ever before. Even if now I was eating shit! Kinda tasty stuff really. Finally for once in my life I knew true joy! Sure did not help me control anything! Knew I was never going back and did not want too! The stress of school and the constant abuse was gone! Mallory was GONE!

Mallory was dead to begin with for the last time! Sorry Chuck.

Athena was here to stay and she was a Happy Dog!

Well I was Athena the Dog damn it and I would bite anyone who ever said otherwise! Laura smiled, shaking her head, as we came in. Becky out of her snow pants and in a short skirt now. "Frankly I have no idea how she got this way Becky? Honestly hunny I think it is just her! She likes being a Dog."

WOOF!

Damn right I did! Laura added. "With what she wrote. I don't blame her."

Becky hugged me. "What's not to like? She is a beautiful, wonderful Dog!" Lifting my snout again to look me in the eye she asked. "You want to have Puppys Girl?" Oh how I did. WOOF! "Well you know how to get them!" Pretty sure she was bored and just wanted a live porn show but I had no problems with being watched. More fun that way even!

Apollo! Romp with him and get him excited. Did not take long before he was trying to mount me. These Boys were just horny! That I was sure was because of me! Three trys but he found the spot and OH WOW! Slam that rock hard Dog-Cock in my Bitch-Pussy hard big Boy! Let me tell you I was panting quick with my joy. My vaginal muscles clamping down hard only increased the sensation. Such fun having that furry body sprawled across my back panting very hard as well. Like he was worshiping me. Giving me his seed!

Laura spoke sounding only mildly disgusted? "Seriously Becky, do you realize how distracting that is?" Ooh! Tell me about it! Nothing else mattered to me right then. Laura was watching now however. Probably blame scientific curiosity! Liar!

Becky was looking at us with such intense lust in her eyes now. Her voice breathless. "Yeah. Isn't it?" Sounded like she wanted something again from me or maybe something more?

Fenrir went next. He hammered me so hard I almost fell. By the time Cerberus was ready Becky was bored perhaps, because she said. "Hump her in the butt Cerberus!" That got Laura's attention again. She liked a good show too it seems. Who doesn't like to watch a good butt fucking? Oh me? A big Slut and I admit it freely! At least now. Maybe I liked the audience reaction. The cheers and encouragement? Took the excitement to new levels I knew. Well I was a Bitch and nothing more! Wiggled for him. Had to shift to get him up there where my Owner wanted him but he did. Right up the poop chute! Becky came over and watched closely on her knees. Practically had her head between us. Once the tie was made Becky said snickering. "Watch this Mom!" Her hand was under me and in my snatch and those pudgy fingers went nuts on my clit! Dogs have them you know. Rapidly I was not able to make an intelligible sound let alone keep standing with those naughty talented pudge fingers having their way with me.

Laura finally said sort of understandably concerned. "You're gonna make her pee on the rug Becky!" She was too and soon. She had a free hand however and she pulled her sweater up and off. No bra! Nice pudgy Tits! This was a very fine ChewToy! Slid the bunched up sweater between us down her arm and held it there against me to catch my urine. Hoped it held it all and I let loose with a whimper. The only thing holding my hindquarters up by this point as my legs were gone was that tremendous shaft inside me still. Legs were just trembling with pure ecstasy! You humans will never know the truth!

May have even passed out for a second as an orgasm hit me. Several times! Oh this was beyond anything so far. Such unbelievable pleasure coursed through me. My mind was just gone. But not far enough that I did not feel Becky lean in and kiss Cerberus tenderly on his stinky pucker before saying. "I'd kiss yours Girl but it's busy. Maybe later?" Might have only been a delusion but I was still hopeful.

Laura laughed joyously. "You are not kissing me again either! Ever!" that I understood. She paused, then said with sudden enthusiasm. "This is quite remarkable. The bots were just supposed to heal damage it says but this has to be them! They seem to think she would be better as a Dog though." Well I agreed! "It is weird! I'm going to fix lunch as I'm hungry. Join me when you can." She got up and came over to lift our tails for a better view. Her voice nonchalant. "That looks kind of painful." And she left. Fenrir followed her wiggling rump. He was alert so maybe he felt something. Maybe he was hoping for a human food treat too! Pretty sure she was a pushover for us Dogs! Let her Daughter practically have sex with us and only watched.

Well I was thinking seriously that Becky caught the pee in her sweater but what about the drool puddle on the carpet? Oh there was one! Turns out I am a drooler. Smelled something good cooking before long which made the drooling worse. Cerberus came out of me with a mighty SLURP and I was flat on the floor. Becky lifted my tail and looked. "Yes that looks very painful. I better kiss it and make it better!" Oh that Girl could kiss ass like a pro or a Dog! Lots of tongue! Knew she tasted Dog cum too. Lots in both holes after all. Maybe she wanted a taste? They both just left me there in an orgasm induced coma! Did she put her sweater back on? Was that what I just saw? Kinky pudge was wearing my pee. Could I wear some of hers?

Came back a few minutes later with a plate. Smelled grilled cheese! Love Grilled Cheese! Offering me one I raised my head. She had to feed it to me as I had no strength left but I ate it. Darn good too. This pudge liked me a lot it seemed. Maybe too much but I was fine with that! Had put the sweater back on too! Yes she was wearing my pee now. Did I own her now? Wondered again if I could wear hers. Might be a Dog thing? Might have wanted to while still human. She is cute.

Outside and potty. The Boys all pooped butt I would need a while as everything had been shoved back in good. Still sniffed and tasted theirs. Rolled in some too. Hey it just happened. Well I did not think let's roll in poop before I just did it. Wondered if my mind would just go total Dog sooner or later? Would I be nothing but a Dog for the rest of my life? Felt some loss at that thought. Hey I had worked hard for some of that knowledge in my head. Would be a shame to waste it. Had some Canine ideas in my head but seemed to still be me so I wondered about it. If I did go total Dog however would I even feel the loss?

Maybe Becky feared the same thing. Her voice happy yet sad she told me. "You will always be treated nice here Girl. We love our Pets."

Laura just rolled her eyes and said. "She needs a bath though and so do you Becky pee-pee sweater!" We did! Knew what was coming next. Followed Becky to the Dog bathroom again with my tongue hanging out all happy like. Definite Dog Thing!

Sat and watched as she got naked for me. She put on a good show for me it seemed. All very wiggly. Sexy stuff! She was a gorgeous pudge after all! Just a slight belly bulge that gave her some curves that just seemed to never end. The patch of strawberry blond between her legs. Red Squirrel! Bigger breasts than mine. Her Mom had some nice ones but Becky was bigger. Opening the glass door for me I went and she followed me in. Realized she would have needed to get naked to give me a shower anyway. She would get wet for sure. Pretty sure she wanted it though and that's why she put the sweater back on.

Humming she got the water started and knelt beside me. It had a long hose hanging down with a big hand held shower head. She switched it over and began soaking me down with warm water. It felt so nice on my skin and in my fur. Fur kind of itches after all. Dry skin ya know. Then again growing fur is an itchy process as well. Setting the hose aside she quickly grabbed the shampoo and we were both sudsy fast. Oh she rubbed on me well. Was not a small Dog after all. She nicely scrubbed both my butthole and cunny well for me. Felt amazing! Well my butt was itchy a lot now since I couldn't wipe anymore. Then she reached under me and scrubbed my breasts. First one then the other then the next? She scrubbed all eight. WHOA! Hey I had eight tits now! Hot Damn! Six of them were just small B cups sure, but I was good. How many of you wish your Girlfriend had eight tits?

Scrubbed her back for her. Hands were definitely paw like but they still worked for this. Used my body a bit as well. Washed her Squirrel while she was straddling me. Using me to wash it. Athena the scrub brush!

Used the side of my head as well. Especially between her legs! Rinse and repeat! Both of us got slippery rubbing on each other. Might have bitten her butt cheek in there too. Hard! She never complained. Just gasped. Left teeth marks I saw. So chewy! This did however make me realize I had a bit of fur. Hindquarters mostly with some up the back and a little starting on my chest. Wondered if I could control the change to an extent. Thought very hard at the silly Nanobots I now knew were in me as I got conditioner applied. Fur was gonna shine.

Was not all pleasant in there as she told me about the first Athena however while we were showering. The Original Dog had been born the same day as her. Her parents had gotten Athena for Becky as a friend, protector, and companion when a Pup. She was a big Chow, Newfoundland mix. Had lived over seventeen years before dying. That was two years ago. Becky and her had been inseparable and Becky cried for three days non stop when she died. Athena had raised the Boys like her own Pups when Becky's Father got them three years ago. Becky was only nineteen now and barely that so younger than me. Athena's death had devastated her completely. Her depression had grown so bad she had tried to take her own life and now I understood her reaction to the name on my tag. Becky rinsed us and toweled us off at least. Could feel her tremendous sorrow and pain still.

She led me back to the Den. Naked! Both of us! As we came in her Mother Laura just shook her head and rolled her eyes but said nothing about it. Becky probably did this a lot I thought from that reaction. The nudity that is. Just a feeling I got. Ever know any little kids that would not keep their clothes on? Becky never outgrew that it seems. Then again I would learn they lived their lives in isolation a lot so it did not matter all that much if she wore clothes. Becky got a Dog brush from a drawer and brushed me. Put my head hair which was still fairly long in a top knot ponytail to keep it out of my face. As the loud very sharp beeping started when she was done she swore. "Shit!"

Laura was up and moving fast very tense. "Stay here!" And she was gone out the door in a flash. Becky held me tight for a couple minutes trembling until. BANG! BANG! BANG! Three quick shots from a rifle. Silence. Becky may have been necking with me in her worry! Very distracting for both of us. Sure felt like she was but I was busy listening. Laura came in with a really nice rifle in her hands. "Seriously Becky? Giving Athena a hickey?" Ooh had she? "Three Men out there. They went back outside the perimeter for now. They will try again though! Damn your Father! Why couldn't he be happy just killing people anymore!" Becky snickered and I got the impression this rant had happened before as well. Many times! Laura looked at her Daughter. "You know I'm right! Make toxic stuff or weapons of mass destruction and no one cares about it! Governments just give you more money! But NOOOO! He had to try and save people. He may not be dead but all those people on that plane are and that is his fault! Positive they saw the cars out there though and know who is here. They will try again. Different tactics but they will." Her voice had been dire. Okay and sarcastic! Suddenly shocked sounding. "Becky! Are those teeth marks in your ass?" Oops! Quick I hung my head. Told ya!

Laughing hard now Laura kinda looked at me and pointed. "She has two cheeks ya know! Now they don't match." True! She does doesn't she?! Very soon it had teeth marks as well. Mom had some kinks too it seemed! Loved her Daughter so much as well! How many of you with teenage Daughters worry every time they go out?

Becky snickered. "Hey Mom watch this!" On hands and knees Becky wiggled her plump rump at the Boys. She was naked and apparently quite horny. Well I sure as heck could smell it! Mounted fast by Apollo who jack-hammered on her plump rump. The look on her face told me what mine looked like at times. Now that was embarrassing! He tried to make the tie but came out when he did. Fenrir did not hesitate going next. Wham bam thank you Ma'am! Her arms and legs were shaking bad so I squeezed under her tits for support. And a taste! Maybe revenge? Cerberus was naughty! He liked the butt it seems and did not hesitate to finish her off that way! That Girl confessed her love for everyone and everything with a big Dog-Cock up her tooter hole! Liked gay porn a lot it seemed! Her Mom looked shocked at most, especially the Gay porn, but still snickered at her Daughters perversions. Felt like the apple had not fallen so far from the tree. Wondered if Becky had ever done this before?

Coming over to get a better look Laura asked. "How does it feel to be a Bitch Becky?" Not an intelligent sound was made. Bit of drool however. Tums out Becky is a drooler as well. Laura lifted Cerberus tail to see better. Liked what she saw it seemed as she smiled. Once he was out of Becky I carried her to the beds on my back and lay her down as an honorary Dog as she deserved that title after that. What about the couch? Dogs are not allowed on the furniture and I planned on cuddling. My pudge! Buried her in Dog body's. Was nap time after all.

We slept for a bit.

Nice to nap on a squishy drooling pudge. Smelled something very good cooking that woke me. Smelled garlic and rather strong. Recalled that Dogs should not have garlic however and I grew sad. Smelled so good though. Got up and Dog-Like padded out to the kitchen. My semen enema was working well now and I had to go rather urgently. Laura was humming while she cooked. In that adorable Yule apron she looked rather cute and Motherly in a very hot and sexy way. She turned and just smiled at me as I came in. Smiled back as I went for the door and trotted outside into the deep snow.

Snow suddenly exploded out beyond the fence and I freaked! Race for the fence barking my fool head off. Laura had the door open with rifle in hand in time to see what caused the fuss. Boys came fast. We watched the Deer I had startled and now scared completely run off through the woods. Laura laughed joyfully. Hey it was Deer! Never got to chase a Deer! Wanted too! Realized I had a long Doggy too do list in my head. Doggy style! Things to chase: Deer, Car, Cat, Bunny, Pudge, Squirrel, Mailman! It's a Dog thing! You wouldn't understand it! The Boys seemed very proud of me though and guarded me enthusiastically from the ferocious Deer while I pooped I think. Maybe the smells I was making had them wanting a snack! Ate it afterwards didn't they. Also a Dog thing. We played in the snow a little before we went back in. Such fun!

Becky was there in a cute short red skirt with a tight orange turtle-neck sweater. All I could think was Velma from Scooby Doo! (Ruhr Roh here comes Shaggy.) She was setting some stuff up carefully on the far counter. Lots of stuff! Smiling at us she asked in a squeaky voice. "You Doggy's wanna help make Christmas cookies tonight?" We all Woofed at that. They knew what a cookie was!

Laura snickered telling us. "After we eat Boys! And Girl." She set our dishes down full of pasta and meatballs and sauce and oh wow! Tails were wagging hard now. "Sit! Wait!" She put their food on the table while we waited all four of us drooling heavily and wagging our tails. Evil Mom! They sat and served themselves before saying grace. Kinda liked it really. It felt like we were a true family.

Not just them. But all of us!

"Eat!" And we were in it. Tasted no garlic in mine but very yummy with lots of oregano! Licked my dish clean. Becky made us beg and jump for extra garlic free meatballs. Playful ChewToy I felt. Got the feeling somehow I was what put a smile on her face right now as her Mom kept looking at her oddly with amazement. Was Becky happy to have a Dog again? Was I a new Athena for her? Yes I would gladly be hers if she wanted me. Forever!

Found somewhere I belong for Christmas!

Kind of understood why Becky might accept me unconditionally as a Dog. Mom Laura was a different story. Sensed a reservation in her. She was willing to do anything for her Daughter but kidnapping and illegal human experimentation was a stretch. Hoped that was all. She was a bit secretive.

Mom mumbled. "Hope the garlic gets rid of your poop breath Becky."

Kind of understood that sentiment.

After they were done eating, took us Dogs ten seconds, we made lots of cookies! Not just human cookies either. The Dog cookies were so delicious. Not to sweet but very yummy! Heavy on the peanut butter! Becky even ate one blushing while her Mom watched. Said it was not bad tasting. Gave us Dogs each a human cookie. Even Laura reluctantly tried a Dog cookie after much prodding from her Daughter. That was so sweet and the Boys liked watching it. Needed frosting she said so we got a simple frosting on ours too! Frosting is Good!

Cookies baked we settled in and watched some Rudolph together. Becky lay on the couch and I lay in front of it getting petted. Not sure when Becky fell asleep but she did. Had an Angelic smile on her face with her hand still on me. Long necks are nice. From the tear visible in her Mothers eye as she looked at us I knew that smile was not normal any more. So I wondered how bad Becky had truly been?

Laura went out and came back with blankets. Putting one on her Daughter gently kissing her forehead she knelt and put a blanket on me. Lifting my snout to look me in the eyes she asked with a tremor in her voice. "Will you be my little Girls pet Athena? Stay with her forever?" So much emotion in that Mother's voice and I knew I understood. Becky had been totally devastated by the loss of her lifetime friend and now I had brought joy back in her life! Nodded well certain of this choice! Wanted it so bad myself now. Was never happy as a human! Felt almost nothing but joy as a Dog! And this Girl was so sweet and held such love in her heart. Knew I could be happy here forever. Was happy here! Leaning in further Laura kissed me gently on the lips. Poopy breath and all. "Eww. Thank you Athena!" Turned off the TV and she left. Heard the Boys snoring but also Becky.

Laying my head down I closed my eyes listening to her cute gentle snores knowing I now had a purpose and an Owner. So much joy at that thought!

Well I was a DOG!

CHAPTER 5 BAD BLOOD Sunday December 23rd

Alarms going off suddenly woke us all! Not quite fast enough! The extremely loud roaring blast of the shotgun a second later was deafening in the house. The roar of his mean voice as he kicked in the shattered front door splintering it apart was even louder. "Where the fuck are you, you filthy lying piece of shit Cunt?!" Knew that voice far to much and I grew scared. "Those fucking Cops you sent to arrest me? They knew you were lying you sack of shit so they fucking told me you were fucking out here and your fucking car is out there so I know they didn't fucking lie! Come out so I can fucking kill you once and for all, you fucking fat ugly fuck whore! Put this shotgun up your nasty fucking Twat and pull the fucking trigger!" He was drunk still. You could hear that in his voice. His words were very slurred. Could also hear murder in that voice. So terrified and just focused on his actually being here it took me a moment to realize the couch was empty. BLAM! Becky yelped in fear somewhere. Not in pain at least! She must have been in the bathroom and gone to see what was happening. "Freeze you fat fucking cum slut! Where is that worthless cunt Mallory?" Now I grew pissed! How dare he call Becky fat! She wasn't and if she was so what. She was mine! All that mattered to me now and my fear rapidly became anger. Had no idea why he ever went out with me other then I was willing to do whatever he asked. All the Girls he cheated on me with were hot skinny things. There were lots of them as well.

The terror in Becky's voice was evident. "Who?" So was the confusion! Well she had no idea who Mallory was. Not sure I did anymore! Knew who Athena was! Athena did not take abuse from anyone!

Us Dogs were cautious but went quick and we split up right away. These Boys were extremely well trained after all. Wondered if they had ever done this before. It was easy to come at the front hall from two different directions. Four actually. Not counting the front door. Pretty much anywhere in the house we could. Heard Becky yelp and him snarling. "You're really a cute little fat fuck whore aren't you? Once I kill that worthless cunt Mallory maybe I can rape your fat ass for a while before I kill you too! Can't leave any witnesses after all! You want my cock in your mouth don't ya Slut?" This Mother Fucker was dead now! Mallory was a wimp. Athena was not! Found my inner Wolf and fear was nothing!

Asshole was turned away from us as we got there. Fenrir did not make a sound next to me but I could feel him tensing at the sight as well. Asshole had Becky facing away from him her back against himself with his left arm around her cute neck and a double barreled shotgun in the other. Wondered if he was sober enough to even reload! Well if not he had nothing in the gun. He looked pissed and Becky looked very terrifyed. He was squeezing her breast telling her how much fun she was going to have with his cock stuffed in her every hole. That if she was a good fuck he might let her live for a while. Of course he was distracted with Becky and thoughts of his tiny cock. Typical Asshole.

Apollo and Cerberus came in the other way and were much better hung then him! Easily spotted however. They just stood there and looked at him. Distracting him? Not angry either. We crept closer from behind. That unfortunately was when Laura spoke up, probably not seeing us, her voice was cold as ice. "Let my Daughter go and leave you Son Of A Bitch or you're going to die!" No. Asshole was not gonna leave! Asshole was just gonna die! She had her rifle pointed at Sphincter Boy. No clean shot however as he quickly shifted to hide behind Becky like the gutless coward I suddenly realized he was. There were four ways into the front hall. Something told me if she had a clear shot Asshole would have just died. Ice Queen would kill without a second thought. Liked her!

Asshole twisted now hiding further behind Becky like the coward he was and his gun turned toward the floor as he did. Everything happened at once very fast. Everyone suddenly moved. His gun came up at Laura and went off. Apollo courageously leapt in front of Laura taking the shot meant for her as I went for the gun arm savagely. Aware of my teeth sinking deep into his flesh and the taste of sweet warm blood in my mouth! Gleefully I just bit harder. Savagely! Fenrir hit him low in the back of the knees and Becky twisted free screaming in terror. "NO!" Lunging for Apollo's bleeding ravaged body where it lay on the floor.

There was blood everywhere however and I grew…Angry! Laura was even hit and bleeding in a couple spots but she moved fast and easy so I knew she was not hurt too bad. Took only two pellets. Bird shot. Not Buck Shot at least! One in the arm, one the shoulder. Opening a small secret drawer on the buffet she pulled out a syringe with a green liquid in it, knelt, and shoved it in his arm. "You can let go now Girl!" She hissed at me grabbing her purse off the buffet and pulled a quality pair of handcuffs out. Cocked my head at her and she blushed. Kinky new Mom! Carried handcuffs. She put them on a wrist and a hook bolt in the floor under the buffet I had not noticed.

Becky's voice held such pain as she held Apollo's bloody body. "He's hurt bad Mom! I think He's gonna die!" Now I looked. Apollo was laying there bleeding badly, whimpering, barely breathing. Hurt bad was an understatement! He had taken most of the blast, meant to kill Laura, saving her life. Such bravery! Such Loyalty! Such is a Dog!

"Can you get him to the car hunny? My arm is a bit rough. It's gonna hurt him when you do but he will die if we don't move fast!" Laura sounded very emotional here as well. Then her eyes going wide looking at me whispering as her face got a smile. "You mad Bastard!" Did not think she meant me. Suddenly she was grabbing coats, boots, and keys! The humans dressed fast now. As Becky carried Apollo's limp form out to the car Laura said sharply. "Cerberus, Fenrir, stay and guard! Athena come!"

Did not understand what was happening but did not hesitate either. My duty was to these people and Apollo. My Pack, My Family! Wondered why Laura still had the gun with her as we went to the car but she knew what she was doing it seemed. Laura drove very fast on rather icy roads. Better then I could that was for sure. Still scared me! Becky was just in tears, her heart broken, holding Apollo. Never had time to think about it but I was still half human and it was noticeable! We pulled into the big vet clinic I had passed on the way out here and they got out very quickly. Laura snapped her fingers commanding me. "Athena! Come!"

Went like a good Dog should! No questions asked! She was the true Alpha! It was Sunday however and the clinic was closed except for emergency's so there were only two cars here. There were people though. Was a big place for sure. More an animal hospital then anything else. Was sure they had Animals who needed tending daily. Even on the weekends. Any boarders had to be fed as well. We went in fast and hard without a care. The yelling began immediately from a plump older Woman. Mostly about the gun! Than she saw me and the screaming started. Understood now why the Boys liked them. Screams are such fun! For one older Woman she could make some noise! True Laura still had the gun and that may have scared her too.

Laura barked at her. Gesturing with the gun for emphasis. Got why she had it still. Hated red tape as well. Apollo would not live if there was any delay here. "Operating room now! Where is it?!"

The Male Veterinarian stepped out from an office and hesitated but a moment as he took it all in. Lots of blood on us so he shouted! "This way!" And he went fast. He was a Vet and Apollo was an injured Dog! That was all that mattered at the moment. Once in the fancy operating room Becky quickly lay Apollo on the operating table properly. Strong girl I thought. He was a very heavy Dog. Well he sat on me so I know. A lot!

Laura quickly pointed at me speaking with tremendous conviction. "We need to transfuse her blood into him or he's dead! No questions now. Just do it!" Had the gun pointed in his general direction after all. Not right at him of course but close enough that he merely acted. He did not seem to care about the gun really. Think I was what was distracting him! Was very interesting looking you see.

He hesitated for only a moment before moving fast which impressed me. Grabbing some equipment he asked while he worked rapidly. "What exactly is she? Is her blood even compatible with him?"

Laura actually snickered at those questions! Knew now she knew something! Or at least suspected. "Nothing but idea's on either really but she may just put you out of business one day! Apollo is dead no matter what unless I am right!" He was nodding at that. He knew Apollo's wounds were fatal just by looking at him! Surprised he was still actually alive it seemed. The original Athena lived seventeen years which is very remarkable for her breed. The Professor had been constantly supplementing all the Dog food for over a decade to strengthen their bodys to live longer. Having put the gun down Laura was helping him very skillfully now. They were putting IV's in us both extremely professionally. Laura knew her way around medical equipment that was certain. The technical stuff they were talking about was beyond me.

Becky still looking so very scared but sounded more curious now as she asked. "What do you mean by that Mom? That she may put him out of work?"

With a very sad smile as she helped the Vet finish hooking IV's on us she told what she suspected as my blood went into Apollo and deep down I knew she almost had the truth. "Your Father actually loves you more than anything else hunny and he is totally insane! That is what it means. Seems he was not as oblivious to the world around him as I always thought he was either. Might have to even apologize to him if he's still alive. He loves you hunny and he loves you so much he was willing to die if he had too to make you happy again." Becky was looking at her Mother like she had gone crazy now. Okay I was too. The Veterinarian worked frantically but was listening intently. Laura's voice grew very gentle as she spoke. "He actually saw how hard it hurt you when Athena died hunny! And here I thought he didn't even notice as he was always so absorbed in his damn work but he really did notice it seems. It was just after she died that he began working on this damned project after all. Actually I should have have been the one to understand right away. All he ever said to me was it was something to heal instead of kill for a change. Was never meant for healing humans though sweety! Only for Dogs! Maybe one specific one! He never wanted to watch you hurt like that again! He was trying to heal you hunny." She was beginning to cry with the memory of her Daughters pain. "What is in Athena here can heal Apollo and so much more! It was all right there in his notes and I was to blind to see it! He created the damned fountain of youth for Dogs! Just Dogs! Very species specific. He must have been afraid they would take it and lock it away without ever understanding. That it would do this to Athena probably never dawned on him though. Not exactly sure why it's acted this way myself. The Nanobots just found themselves in a body that was not right as far as they knew so they fixed it! She was not a Dog after all and that was what they were supposed to do so they have been remaking her on a genetic level into a real Dog!"

Stopping the transfusion with a clip the Vet looked quite nervous at all this information. "She actually used to be human?" We all nodded. He looked horrified. "Does she want to be a Dog?" Damn right I Woofed and nodded. Damn right I did even if I lost my mind I would be happy with them here. Going back would never be an option for me! My Family!

Laura sighed shaking her head telling the Vet. "She even wants Puppys too. No idea if she ever can have them but for her sake I hope so!" Tears were running down Laura's face as she spoke. Apollo was already stable now and breathing much better. This totally amazed the Vet of course! Explanations of injury's were given as bird shot was dug quickly from Apollo's chest wounds. Becky helped Laura dig the shot from her arm and shoulder at the same time. Well Veterinarian's can not work on humans! And I learned an awful lot about myself. They told him how the Professor slipped the Bots in my drink to save them from whoever. Not quite true though now was it? Well I had been set up. The Veterinarian learned too and seemed totally fascinated with what he heard.

My old life was told to him as well and he said petting me. "You're safe now Girl! These are good people!" Had the idea they knew each other to an extent. Not well but enough. This was probably where the Boys came for check-ups and vaccinations. Yes for people who created such nasty instruments of death for the military my people were GOOD PEOPLE! Explained where the money came from. Both the Professor and Laura were scientists who made weapons for the military. Biological, Chemical, and others. Well until the first Athena died. It was then he just quit and started the road to me! Laura told the Doctor what she suspected. Her husband had been truly devastated by Becky's grief. He had created an animal specific healing tool. Why he gave it to me was not known for sure. Best guess he did not want to lose it and being animal specific he may have thought it would lay dormant in me till he could get some out. Made sense to us even if we were wrong! Unfortunately or maybe not it did not stay dormant. Suspected my injury's activated them but that was wrong as well. They had no intelligence so they thought! And the bots assumed I was just a deformed Dog! Started to fix me! (Always knew I was broken.) (Never knew I was supposed to be a Dog!) Owed the Professor. Yes even I saw this as an improvement. It really fixed me! My body was never right after what my Sister and Father had done to me. Now I mostly hoped it fixed certain parts of me. Really wanted those Puppys! If I lost my intelligence but could actually have Puppys I thought I would still be happy!

Individually the Nanos had no intelligence! Together? Perhaps not. A part of me had wanted each of these changes I now knew. Had thought about a tail after all and I got one. Had thought shorter legs and got them. Thought fur and got it. My hind quarters looked sorta canine but I still had my big round human butt. Looked adorable with fur on it. Paws in back where my feet once were but kinda hands up front still. Very short fingers but usable. Wanted more fur yet as without it I got cold but my skin tingled a lot so I figured it would be soon. If I went all Dog? Even my mind? Well I was loved here!

"That is so amazing! If I was not seeing it I would not believe it!" The Veterinarian exclaimed. He had finally finished fishing the shot from Apollo and was examining the wounds. "They are healing already! This is so impossible! Everything you said was real?!" Did not blame him for his skepticism. He looked at me with awe now.

The transfer of my blood had been stopped rather quick but we were still hooked up just in case Apollo needed more I assumed. Seemed unnecessary now. As Laura finally unhooked me she asked the Vet. "When can Apollo come home?"

He seemed flustered by that question. "Well it would be safer for him if he stayed medically but as he may be a potential target here I would rather he go home with you now! No offense. My safety you see is not important but there are several innocent animals here who could get hurt if something happened. Some of my employees may not keep it a secret either. Greed is in everyone after all. It is unbelievable what I have seen and I want to tell the world myself! Fortunately I have better control then most and can wait. What you have said and I have seen is fantastic and I hope to retire soon! Keep me informed please. I'll come check on him later if I can even though I suspect he will be fully healed by then. Really would like to see some of the research soon." He was wrapping some gauze around Apollo's chest. He seemed nervous. "Um I don't know if it's safe but did you want to get her vaccinated now? If she is going to be a Dog she will need them after all."

Laura looked thoughtful. Oh I was nervous now. Did not like needles much. You should have seen the ones they stuck in me in the hospital after what my Sister did?! Laura's voice was gentle as she spoke. "We really probably should now shouldn't we? There is a high potential for contact with the public and police so yes! Can you do it for us?"

Now I was just shaking. Becky noticed this however and quickly held me while he shoved that huge thing into my rump! Okay I admit I am a coward at times. Never saw the second needle coming so I yelped! Gave him a stern look!

"That was a distemper shot hunny. You will need a Parvo shot by spring!" We had told him what happened to get us here of course. "I've been thinking though. About the guy who shot Apollo? Now I can't help you there myself but I do know someone who might be able too." He wrote a name and a number on some paper. "He drove there right?" Nodding. "My Wife is Guido's cousin. They were at our wedding. Nice people for mobsters really. Tell them the truth. Just not on the phone! Tell him on the phone you have a vehicle needs disposed of immediately and someone will come get it for you. Whatever is in the trunk will be disposed of as well no questions asked.”

Got the feeling he really would have liked to help us as his reaction at hearing about Dickhead was bad. Did not like people who shot Dogs it seemed. Or beat on Women for that matter. Really liked this Vet. Certain he had wanted to get samples from me he didn’t. Not a stupid greedy man. Just very curious. We promised to keep him informed. Might be useful someday.

It was just after noon by the time we got back home. Asshole was still there whimpering in his own blood. Smelled like pee as well. Cerberus’s to be exact. Owed him now too. Could tell each Dogs scent easy now after all. Seemed really easy and I kinda wondered why I never could before. In the torn flesh of Dick’s arm there was pee as well as most other places. Hope it burned the bastard. Apollo had actually walked into the house by himself by God. Not fast yet but he would be fine soon. By the time Dick was fully conscious they had him tied in a nice dining room chair very secure. Only chair they could move except the desk chair and Laura said the Professor would freak if we used it. Also more comfortable than one of these. Might be a Louie the 14th chair? No idea what one looks like! Solid yet fancy chair. Laura had a large black case open on the buffet already with an extremely scary nasty look on her face. Gagged now he could not speak. Or scream. Just watch in horror at what was coming!

Laura put on a thick gray glove that looked like something a hockey player wore but this one was humming? Was that the glove? Something was humming I heard. Becky was cutting all of Assholes clothing off quite happily. My ChewToy had a nasty streak! Oh I liked that. That glove was very special I could already tell and knew Dickhead was going to hate it. Laura leaned in to his face. Her voice was so sexy I got turned on by it. “You like it when Girls touch you down there?” He slowly nodded without a clue. “Want me to touch you down there?” He hesitated getting scared more than angry. She reached down and stroked him gently with her bare hand. Saw he was getting hard quick now. “Think you could actually satisfy me with this?” Quick arrogant nod then his hope came crashing down and I got a thrill. Her face still happy she switched hands. “With this tiny little prick? You have got to be kidding me!” He was trying to rip that chair apart he was struggling so hard! You did not insult his manhood! Even if it was true. Watched him put two guys in the hospital once for it. ZZZZAPT! Oh that looked painful! Much more than a taser! Convulsions look a lot like rage still only the eyes roll back in the head or you can not tell the difference. Smelled the burning flesh and I smiled. Barbecued wiener anyone? That glove packs one hell of a punch it seems! Looked like it damn near killed him. Laura’s voice was so sweet but evil as she said to her Daughter while looking at him! “Becky dear? You know? I think his nipples are uneven. Be a dear and get the pliers. See if you can fix them for him.” Such joy they were having torturing this piece of excrement. Oh they tortured too.

Was quite proud of my humans you see! Was their Dog now so they were My Humans! Even if they were bloodthirsty mass murderers! Then again Dog's morals are not yours. They tortured him badly for a while. Maybe half hour. Think he was begging to die now. Felt sad he was gagged as I wanted to hear those words on his lips. Oh we missed all those fun screams of pain and horror that Dogs love! Had sat where he could see me the whole time. He stared at me when he was able to. Laura finally ripped the gag off him as she thought he was tenderized enough to talk and snarled. "Who told you Mallory was here?!"

Spluttering he stammered in pain. "T-T-two C-Cops! They showed up last night and said she was pressing obviously false rape and assault charges on me! That I was going to end up in prison if she didn't drop the charges!" My God! Was he serious? Was he that damn stupid?

Laura scoffed her voice full of disgust. "God you really are an idiot! So these two Cops just told you where she was? Basically told you to shut her up?" How would Cops know where I was? Not Cops I knew.

No idea when he noticed who I had been but he grabbed at a straw. "Help me Mallory baby! You know I love you!"

Becky said it so very, very cold amazing me as I sat there staring at him and drooling. "Mallory is dead Asshole! Meet Athena!" Somewhere in that Girl the primal Lizard brain rose! Definitely her Mother's Daughter! "You are never going to hurt any Girl again! Not with that!" She pointed at his still somewhat hard cock! Assume it was the electric shocks kept it hard. No idea otherwise. "Athena? Fetch the little stick!" So cold she said it it sent a thrill up my spine. Me! Hey I was hot and passionate letting all my savage anger out now! That stick was mine damn it! Dogs like to fetch sticks! Carried away however and I swallowed. Damn nasty really so I followed Cerberus out back and we ate each others poop to get the taste out of my mouth while Dickwad just bled to death all over the floor. That poop had a much better taste then his stick.

Once back in we saw Laura was on the phone already. Her voice rather delightful sounding, having a nice conversation with something. Sounded like she had just watched her Daughter command me to kill. Becky had the mop and a bucket watching him bleed out all the way just smiling. "Well thank you sir and we will see you soon." Laura scratched my ears. Ahh! Oh that is so, so wonderful! "That wasn't very much to eat at all Athena. I bet you're still hungry Girl aren't you?" All four of us Dogs Woofed. To the kitchen! A Dogs favorite room.

It was a nice quick lunch as it was lunch time already.

He was dead when we all came back. About fucking time! All three Boys peed on him. Becky began mopping up blood and pee happily. Laura looked at me nervously. "Athena girl?" Alert at that tone. This was important. "Is there anything out in your car you want to keep?" Oh that was all she wanted to know now. Understood what she was getting at so I thought hard. Not really any stuff. Had nothing I needed now. Clothes were useless. What little I owned I might want I could not use. Even stuff at the apartment. Nothing I owned had good memory's attached. Best if Mallory disappears without a trace forever. So I shook my head. Dogs have no need for STUFF! Unless we can chew on it! Then It IS OURS! Those things we wanted and kept! That was what Becky was for though.

WAIT! Was something important in there though. Did not need it anymore myself but it really should not go to waste I felt. Saw homeless people all the time. Made eating motions at the floor then point with my snout Saying. "Ood." Best I could manage with floppy lips! Try talking without your lips and see how you sound sucker!

Becky got excited. Well she understood. "You never had much to eat in the pound did you Girl?!" Hard to snicker without lips either! Did anyway.

Laura seemed to get it. "You don't want the food in the car to go to waste?" Hard to nod and snicker at the same time as well for a Dog I find.

Hearing the tow truck show up coats were grabbed by humans and out we went in time to see a dashing fancy dressed average size man with slicked back black hair get out of the passenger side of the imposing vehicle. Sasquatch was getting out of the drivers seat. Six foot six at the least. Over three hundred easy. No fat! Every seam on his clothes looked like they were about to explode. All muscle too! Make a good pro wrestler. Might have been one. Both were smiling quite nicely however as they came over. Seemed extremely friendly for sure but they seemed dangerous as well. Could just tell by how they moved. Like real jungle predators. They could kill if they had too and I knew it. These were not the kind of Men you crossed. Definitely the kind of men could dispose of a stray body for you however! The smaller dapper Man came over and bowed slightly. "Good afternoon Ma'am, I am Tony the Squid. This 'Thing' is my associate Guido the Sledge." Saw his massive hands and thought I could see where Guido got that name but where did Tony get his? "You said on the phone that you had a car you needed to be removed from the property?" Those names however kinda sounded familiar to me here. Laura held her hand out and he took it raised it to his lips and kissed it gently as the Ladys both introduced themselves. He was a real genuine old world charmer. Guess in his line of work you had to be.

Laura tittered. Well I think it was a titter. "Um actually we have a second vehicle if your interested as well. It's clean." She pointed at my car. "It's not much but everything in both is yours as well. However we have is a slight problem. Some trash still in the house we need to get rid of. It's still in the hall and too heavy for us

Ladys to carry out without messing up the floor." Her voice was pleasant and matter of fact as she eyed Sasquatch and Tony quickly smiled. She led the way in and they followed. Watched them closely as they walked. Well I wanted to know how to walk like a Jungle Cat!

They did not bat an eye! At the body or me and that I tell you said loads. Well I was definitely NOT a full Dog! Knew those names from somewhere but my brain was kinda fuzzy still. Yes, I expected to become just a Dog soon. Shrugging Tony said like it was really nothing. So nicely too. "I'm sure he deserved it and all but you Lady's don't want any DNA left around to potentially incriminate you. So where exactly are the missing bits?"

Becky snickered sweetly petting me. "They won't ever find it. They never check Dog poop for DNA!"

Tony just smiled at that and a genuine smile too. He found that actually funny! Yeah I liked him. Guido who had been very nervous and looking hard the whole time at me said. "Boss that ain't no Dog there!"

No idea if he was just teasing the big guy but with a straight face he said. "Well of course she ain't no Dog. These nice Ladys here are Witches and they turned a Girl into a Dog to get her car. This guy tried to stop them and they did this to him!" Guido looked very scared at this. Might puke soon? A Dog can hope too! Trying so hard not to laugh myself. "Just eat or drink nothing here and you'll be fine right Ladys?"

Even nodded myself at this. Most found it hard to keep a straight face I think. Guido finally said still very nervous. Maybe he was trying to change the subject? "Nice chair there. Seems a shame to throw it out."

Laura smiled sweetly at him. Perhaps a little wickedly. "I have seven more if you would like them." That made Guido smile happily now. Bribe or gift it was a moot point as Laura added. "Not sure if you can ever get the blood stain out of it though."

Guido smiled big now. He had a friendly smile. "Not gonna. Best part is the stain! Gonna tell people its the chair old man Tarker got whacked in!" Holy Shit! Now I remembered where I knew the names from! These guys were definite Mob! Tarker, a union boss had disappeared a few years ago. His body showed up weeks later mangled and tortured and it was in all the papers. He had been killed very nasty. These two were both listed as prime suspects at one point. Cold blooded killers were in our house! Some Mobsters too. Cool!

Tony just laughed at his friends words. He had a rather friendly almost musical laugh for a cold blooded murderer.

Becky all sweet asked Tony curiously now. "Mr. Tony? Where did you get the name Squid from?" He only chuckled at the question as Laura stiffened. Well

Laura obviously knew the names as well. The question did not bother him however. The true answer was a different story.

Snickering Guido told getting his revenge. "In forth grade he could not keep his hands off of Kelly Martin. He was all hands too and Kelly named him that! It sort of stuck! He still calls her sometimes too."

Still Smiling, only not friendly any more, Tony said sweetly but not. "You know if I thought it would hurt I'd shoot you Guido!" Guido just smiled at that. Got the feeling their whole relationship was like this. Each trying to out do the other. Get one over on them. Practical Joker Gangsters?! The Abbot and Costello of organized crime! Liked them more.

Becky said quickly remembering before they left. "Oh there's some food in the one car. Can you be nice and give it to someone who could really use it? Shame to see it go to waste! Could help someone here at Christmas time." Tony nodded very nicely at that. Seemed like nice people really. Smelled like it. Not all criminals are bad people and not all Cops are good!

Guido was hooking Dick's car up to the winch as Tony looked intensely at me. Right in the eye and asked serious. "I have to ask you Ma'am." He looked at me. "You like being a Dog?" Nodded well for him. Not so serious now. "You like sniffing butts?" His voice got a different tone I noticed but I nodded. He was gesturing at Guido who was bent over in the other direction. Now I got it! He was so evil! So was I! Snout Goosed Sasquatch!

Deer ten miles away ran in terror at that scream! Tony almost peed himself he laughed so hard! They were rather nice for gangsters! Not like in the movies but real people. Okay maybe like in the movies! Marx Brother's Movies! Hey you know where you stand with the Gangsters at least! Politicians and big business? Good luck there! Becky asked what they were doing for Christmas sounding interested in their lives. Hey who doesn't want to know what killers do for Christmas? Tony said they usually did very little since they came here. Had no Family in the immediate area! They were not very popular. Even with their own associates it seemed. Perhaps because they were not very serious? Liked them myself. We wished them well and they went with the chairs. Good thing we were not expecting company for Christmas huh?

Becky looked at her Mom quite seriously. Some concern in her voice as she asked and I understood what she meant. "We owe them a favor now?"

Her Mom answered sweetly and very Motherly. "Of course we do hunny. Your Father and I owe a lot of people favors. Many owe us. It is the way of the world. We will do what we can for them if they need it within reason." They talked while they cleaned up the last of the evidence. Guido had told us how so the DNA was not recoverable. Well I got attacked and violently stabbed by Cerberus of the large cock! Well Apollo had been shot recently so he couldn't mount me yet!

Speaking of Apollo though. Laura knelt down in front of him and kissed him on the mouth nicely while Cerberus made the tie and squished his big leathery black balls on my left cheek. Feels so cool. "You saved my life Apollo! Now I owe you a lot it seems. Maybe later if your feeling up to it Mommy can start to repay you properly."

"MOM!!!!" Quietly I snickered at the shocked look on Becky's face as she screamed that. She had no room to talk now did she?

Laura grinned at her Daughter saying. "You had your fun with them now didn't you Daughter of mine?" Becky blushed now! Revenge is sweet! Again I snickered. Apollo deserved it! He had been willing to die for her! The least she could do was let him hump her! Very nice really. Knew she would enjoy it. "Don't worry I'll turn on the cameras in my bedroom so you can watch in the morning." Did not think it possible but Becky blushed very well and so much harder! Was she a nympho porn addict? Got that feeling! Knew she liked Gay porn a lot. However I was kinda full of Dog cock at the moment so who was I to say anything? Okay I barked out. "Thank You!"

Being a Dog sort of opened my eyes. They may not have had far to go in many ways. Love and Loyalty are feelings and darn good ones! Sex like peeing and pooping is a bodily function and an action. Generally a very pleasant one too. Not that pooping or peeing especially first thing in the morning is not a pleasant relief. Some mornings darn near as good as sex! Oh do not deny it we have all been there! That awesome relief! Now I bring that up because I had not realized before the tie that I had to go. Was not sure at this point I could hold it for twenty minutes either. Might need another bath!

Laura said rather excitedly. "I'm not cooking! Who wants what on their pizza? I'm having Mexican!" So we had pizza's coming. Three meat lovers, a supreme, and two Mexicans one no onion and extra bacon. Take a guess? Onions are bad for Dogs! Love Mexican Pizza!

At least I got to poop before the pizzas arrived. Cerberus did to so I had an appetizer. Oh you love it when I talk about eating poop and you know it! Okay I admit I liked it a lot. Flavor was flavor! Good or bad I wanted to taste it! It's a definite DOG thing!

Ate pizza! Good stuff. So many flavors I tasted in it now! Oh my sense of smell and taste were off the Leash!

After eating we sat and watched more Christmas shows. The original Grinch and not that horrid movie that ruined the whole story! They said it too. Becky was on the floor with us Dogs cuddling and brushing us. Laura came down and sat with us as well while she brushed Apollo. Hey I had more fur now! Cool! Or would that be Warm! Long thick lush red fur. Looked part Irish Setter for certain! Was a very pretty Girl! Still looked human in a way. Chest had rounded a bit but the face was still mostly mine with a snout. Breasts had shrunk a bit. Had eight now though and they kind of evened out! Brain was still being weird. Seems I was not losing myself so much as gaining more and it had taken time to sort and process. Everything seemed to still be there in my head but now I had more. Knowledge, emotions, thoughts. Not so much becoming a Dog as merging with one! Hmm. Maybe?

It was late when Laura finally said. "I'm ready for bed."

Becky looked at her Mom sheepishly and nervously asked her Mother. "Mom? Can the Dogs sleep with me tonight? Kinda don't want to be alone after today. Really scared me."

Laura got a sad look on her face like she was about to break her Daughters heart. Her voice held such sorrow. "No hunny!" Becky frowned quickly. Laura grabbed Apollo's collar and smiled at her Daughter. "The others maybe but Mr. Stud Muffin here has a new Bitch to pound tonight!" He sure looked happy!

Becky looked absolutely shocked at this. Her voice held astonishment! "You're really gonna let him do you?" Had she doubted her Mothers words earlier? Oh she had thinking her Mom was just picking on her. Apollo was certainly game! Seems he knew who he was mating with tonight.

Laura got up and wagged her ass all the way out calling lustfully for Apollo. He followed that ass, head held high! "Orgy in my bed I guess." Gushing Becky said so very happy now. Would have been crowded with five of us in there. Some one would have had to stand around waiting a turn also. Becky had a very cute and nice room and big bed! Cerberus took Becky like a Bitch in heat in her own bed and he plowed her good. She whimpered and howled for him like a proper Bitch should. He loved it. Fenrir shoved his cock in me and I clamped down hard. Becky could not hold Cerberus in for long to the disappointment of both. She knew he was not done squirting however so she got her head under him and began sucking that massive red rocket! Let me tell you that Pudge can deep throat some huge Dog-Cock! Could not get his bulb in her mouth but she tried quite greedily. Fenrir kinda snickered at it. He had a point. My Owner was a total cock-sucker! Was that what she watched the Gay porn for? Pointers? Becky was not done either! We took turns licking Dog cum from her plump pussy making her squeal on Cerberus cock. Cerberus wanted to show Becky she was his though so he lay down on her face pushing even his mighty bulb into her mouth. Got nervous at that and watched, but he made the tie with her face so he could lick her out too and she could smell his powerful stinky farts. He did it twice right in her face and she had no choice but to breath it in. Had a little difficulty breathing it seemed but not bad.

Looked like she was pretty happy to me.

His cock came out eventually but he did not move. Well she was not letting him. She liked his farts too it seemed. They are mighty nice. He shrugged and lay down atop her and slept. Fenrir and I both slept between Becky's legs as we loved her farts. It is a DOG thing you know!

CHAPTER 6 LAST MINUTE SHOPPING Monday December 24th

Woke very happy! And quite furry finally. Yes! My B-cup breasts butt and face were very furry now, yet looked rather human still! However mostly I was a Dog now. Well I knew! Knew I was done as well. The bots had listened to me it seemed. Or did I have control all along? Interesting idea. Still had stub fingers but at a distance or a quick look I was only a Dog. Odd looking sure but still a Dog. Doggy fingers of course with long Dog nails but functional at least. Could flex them at will so I could grab or type with them still. My tracks would look a bit bizarre in the snow but that was okay.

Had to go potty though. Woke them Boys up and we herded a naked Becky outside to squat in the snow like a Bitch. Made her sniff and taste ours before we let her back in. So we were forcing her to be a Dog. She wanted to be one and did not try to stop us. Yes there was pooping! Wanted to be a Dog? We would make her one! The Boys had made me do it. She asked expectantly as we headed back in. "Am I an official Dog? One of you now?" We Woofed. She was as far as we were concerned. We could take her in the Pack! She was comfy! And tasty! And…

Went in the house and she stood up and ran to grab a robe and a camera quickly. Dogs are curious about everything so we followed her and we were so glad we did! She pushed her Mom's bedroom door open very quietly. Laura and Apollo were sound asleep. Both naked and going 69. She was awesomely sexy. Apollo's snout was in her crotch. Pressed tight in there she was nuzzling his genitals. His leathery nuts were pressed to her lips. Pictures were taken rapidly. Many angles. Well Daughters can be perverts as well as Dogs. Potential blackmail material on Mom as well! Blackmail is fun! You know? Mom say's let's see this movie but You want to see a different one? Or Mom say's No fucking the Dogs in the kitchen while she's trying to make breakfast! Might need it soon for that last reason. Damn I was horny.

We woke them up the best way! Laura squealed loud and jumped. "Get that nose out of my butt!" Had just been outside now hadn't we so my nose was extra cold you understand!

Becky snickered pushing in more. "You smell so nice Mom!" Hers was cold too. Then she licked her own Mom's butthole. Got a gasp now.

Laura's hand whipped back and grabbed Becky's head. Holding her there she said angry. "I dare you! Do that again!" So Becky did! Different tone of voice now! "Oh it feels nice!" Gasp. "Are you trying to taste my shit?" Well she had tasted ours so why not her Mom's as well.

Laura quickly said she had to go potty though. Becky quickly got her a robe and slippers before we herded a laughing Laura outside to squat in the snow. We let her have a robe! Made her taste and sniff Apollo's potty. Not hard to get her to do it either it seemed. Wondered if she had already tasted. Naughty Mom! Well he sniffed and ate hers. We all had a taste. She kissed him afterwards even. With Tongue! She was still alive because of him! Inside she made breakfast for us just a singing. Put Becky's plate on the floor next to my bowl. Made Becky eat there naked. Becky did not mind eating off the floor or being naked! They lived in this house her whole life and keeping clothes on her never seemed worth it. It was a playful atmosphere than. Everyone was happy for the moment. Very strange to me to be in a house full of nothing but joy but I loved it. No one was yelling or throwing things at me! Pleasant.

Once done Laura even let the five of us lick the dishes and pans clean while she said. "Let's get dressed so we can go do some last minute shopping, Becky." Smack on Becky's naked tushy. Smack again. Becky looked at her Mom. "What can I say hunny you have such a nice butt!" She totally did. Laura even groped her Daughters naked butt playfully the whole way up the stairs.

We followed so I know what happened. Not in a hurry after all it seems. Watched while Laura got revenge and raped her Daughter with a vibrator. Well Becky was saying No, Stop, and Don't a lot. Well till the first orgasm. It was early and Christmas eve so the Mall did not open till eleven so we had time. Male Dogs raped us. No complaints there. Just three Male Dogs fucking three willing Bitches! Cerberus mounted Becky and hammered that big throbbing cock in her till that hot pudge drooled! Laura watched that as Fenrir took her sweet backside and plowed it hard. Apollo pounded me right in Laura's face. She said angry yet breathless. "You two timing Bastard! Fucking that hot gorgeous Bitch in front of me!" Yeah don't believe her! She licked his cum from my pussy when he was done. Licked Cerberus's semen from her Daughters snatch with me as well. Becky licked Fenrir's from her Mom. This Family was going with the Dogs! He He. Hornyness makes you do things you would not do otherwise. Like eat out your own Mother. Just an example! Oh it happens. Well I watched it! For most people it does. Yeah she did and we watched. Sex is Sex people and something to be enjoyed and not to be hidden or avoided! Or worse Politicized!

Beats boredom any day!

Hey! I just remembered it was Christmas Eve and knew the mall did not open until eleven today. Well I had not thought of that yet! Mentioned it earlier so you knew why the humans did not seem to be in a hurry. Plenty of time for a good old fashioned orgy filled with Beastiality, incest, and joy! It's fun! Not legally incest either! Sex and Love are two entirely different things! Don't believe me? Never had sex with some one you barely knew? (Sorry that was really mean of me! I know most of you have never had actual sex with a real Woman and that is fine. Do you love your inflatable Girlfriend? We know you love your Inflatable Sheep Steve! Who let him read this? Seriously!)

Clothes on for the humans then boots and coats and they were ready to go. Wow they take forever! So much easyer being a Dog! We were always ready to go! Us Dogs sat in the middle of the front hall waiting to say bye. Laura quickly smiled at us as she stood in the front door holding it open. "Well come on! We can all go shopping!" Oh YES! We charged out to the car like the second coming. Becky jumped in back and the Boys swarmed on her. She makes a good seat cushion. Oh I know! No sex but snouts got shoved many places. Well they were Dogs. Which of course meant I got to ride shotgun. Darn we forgot the Assholes shotgun! Laura nicely rolled the window down for me. The Boys would keep Becky warm. Scratch that one off my Doggy to do list! Oh the pure joy of cold wind flapping your lips! Can not describe it. All those smells shoved down your nose at high speed were absolutely amazing. Bet you never thought about this? How I loved being a DOG!

Those of you who have or had a Dog will understand a bit of this and say. "Now I know why!" Being a Dog is wonderful! Gross from your point of view but a Dog thinks everything is interesting! Ever pull quills out of your Dogs snout? More than once? Or they like to go out and play with the Skunk as well? Knew I owed the Professor my very life big time. No idea if he was alive however so no idea if I would ever get to thank him. Kind of a mix of emotions there. Well I wanted him alive to thank him but worryed if he were alive he may be upset with me having had sex with his Wife and Daughter! Oops! You can understand that one I hope! Hoped he forgave me for any future indiscretions too. Oh I had plans. Sleep, eat, potty, and fuck are what matters most to a Dog! Especially eating fat pudge butt!

Had plans on being a bad Dog as well. My new sense of smell demanded I stick my snout in every butt and crotch I could. Was not arguing with it. May even have been, maybe, encouraging it but I admit nothing. Yes I was a Dog now and it is what Dogs do! You can not believe the things I can smell with my snout in your butt! Know what you had for breakfast! Yesterday. We were told to get out and potty in the Mall parking lot. Yeah, public pottying! Always wanted to do that! Yes even as a human! No idea why. It was just always there in my head.

Laura had some devious plans as well it seemed. Us Dogs looked at the car expecting to get back in when Laura turned to the entrance smacked her leg and said. "Come!" Followed gladly but was amazed by this. All four of us Dogs! Dogs are not allowed in the Mall, right? Sniffed several butts in the parking lot on the way in making some Shoppers squeal. Not just me either. Becky tried to sniff a big Woman and her Mom yelled at her. Big Woman just snickered. Must have kids. Mall security looked intently at us as we came in but they said nothing. Seemed odd to me they let us in and I was confused. Us Dogs were very well behaved but still? Had fun walking through mall as a Dog though. Almost completely naked! Had a collar on! The smells in here were beyond belief. Knew why we had not been stopped by Mall security finally! Well He was here! Santa! Was apparently a special day for bringing pets as we saw a few. YEAH! We got our pictures taken with Santa Clause! My furry tits and all! Okay my tits were a bit floppy and may have looked like I had Pups not long ago. Santa however was a naughty Santa and sorta squeezed one. Probably still give himself a present! Got my revenge however. Shoved my snout in his crotch so hard he cryed. He had to go take a little break then and I just followed him! Felt really bad you see. Did not want to hurt him bad. Just let him know he was naughty. Did not think he was the real Santa either but why take the chance of ruining Christmas. He looked at me terrifyed in the back room when I came trotting in. Wanted to just say I was sorry! Sure he looked scared. Until I turned away from him looked back and cocked my tail to the side panting and than he smiled. Big nasty smile. Santa needs dirty Dog sex too you know! Mrs. Clause is so busy he never gets any fat ass old Lady sex around Christmas.

Santa got the idea real fast and I got the north pole quick! It was a pole to. Santa was well hung. Did Santa do porn in the off season? Promised me a bone for Christmas. What did he call this? Felt like a bone to me! Laura, Becky, and the Boys got pictures taken with the Elf while we were busy. She was a bit plump and so hot looking and most of us thought she would be fun to unwrap under the tree tomorrow. A short red headed pudge named Tara Elf. Laura was smiling at her well when the Elf was not looking, as she kept texting or something on her phone. Knew she was up to something. Dogs are amazingly curious.

That Elf was so sad to see us go finally I thought she may cry. May have just been because it was a slow day but I thought otherwise. She smelled lonely. Well I had stuffed my snout in her crotch too. Three times as a matter of fact. She liked it a bit. Elf Slut? My favorite kind of Elf! She oh so sweetly yet desperately offered to watch us Dogs while the humans shopped. Turned out it was slow and she was bored but really liked us. Santa was fine with it now as well. He had some Dog-Pussy after all. Maybe hoping for more? Well I was good!

The Elf had said rather sadly finally we could help cheer her up for a while if we stayed as she was spending the holiday break home alone once again. She was eighteen and a Highschool senior. All her friends, the three of them, were leaving for the week as had her parents. She had a terrible fear of flying it seems so stayed home. Alone! Wondered as I sat there pretty if she was afraid of being tossed in a car trunk and Kidnapped? Or ravaged by Dogs? No idea on the first yet but think the second was a definite yes! Then again it felt like she was already ravaging us. Yes she poured her heart out to us while groping us and we felt her sadness. All us Dogs did. Dogs are so amazing! You can never truly know! Began thinking of ways to help this poor Elf. Into my Dog dish!

Big shot? Mall employees came to say we Dogs had to go after a little while. Stuck up mid-level employees. Well nobody important was working today. My Elf pudge just frowned and said kinda angry taking out her emotions on them. "You see that nice line of customers? They all want pictures now. With the Dogs! Yes these Dogs! Otherwise we were dead." He apparently did not believe her so he went and nervously asked some of the people in line. There were plenty. They loved us. We were so adorable! The Elf had put big ribbons on us. Santa was also very happy with this arrangement. Got to grope me more. What a pervert. Lots of cute hottys sat on his lap with us Doggys. They smelled nice. Yes a Dog can smell if you're horny or don't wipe well. They can smell your poop butt even if you think you wipe the best. They like that about you however. The stinkier the better!

Smells are everywhere and Dogs smell them all. It is so cool being a Dog! The Elf bought us Dogs lunch. Was not cheap either I knew but she seemed so happy to do it. Such a sweet Elf Girl and we showed her Canine affection. Maybe she seldom got that in her life too. So nice of a Girl really. Felt truly sorry for her as she seemed just so sad and lonely. No one should be alone on Christmas Damn It! Knew what it was like! Then again I thought we may be kidnapping her soon so she might not be alone! Laura was definitely up to something. No I was not sure but it did smell like it was gonna be a kidnapping. Hey my smeller was very good now. Could always make sure though couldn't I? Could still use a phone! Or a computer! Sneaky Dog!

Bad Doggy too!

Okay I have to guess at this stuff I'm about to tell you as I was with the Elf smelling customer's butt's joyfully and not present but Laura and Becky had lots of fun shopping it seemed. They bought some sexy stuff for each other in the naughty store. Also they bought some stuff for me and the Boys. Lots of big full shopping bags in their hands when they came back. The Elf sadly kissed us all as we left her.

Swung by the grocery store real quick. Stayed in the car now! Could not go in here. Laura ran in and came out with several bags. Smelled meat in them! All us Dogs were drooling the whole way back to the house with that smell. Got back to the house and... OH LOOK A SQUIRREL! Off like a shot! Out the open window. Face first! Chase! Sniff! Hunt! Everything was in by the time I came back so I knew it had been a while. Almost had that Squirrel too! The Boys gave me crap for not getting it though! All the way through the house. Then they gave me more crap out in the back yard. That was tasty crap. Smelled meat cooking. Oh I was definitely a drooler like Cerberus! Puddle on the floor time.

Made me hungry so I helped rape a pudge on the kitchen floor. Okay we got yelled at by Mom for doing it in the kitchen and chased our victim to the den fast. No idea what she was screaming so it may have been rape. She was ours though. Fenrir in her! Me laying on my back beneath her just licking her clit for all I was worth! May have peed in my mouth. Tasty pudge! She was panting and smiling once we were done. Covered with slobber and semen bare naked but we were happy Dogs so we were good. All of us sitting on our victim when Laura came in. Almost did not see her Daughter under us so she looked around.

Never batted an eye at the sight though. "Supper is ready." We were off like rockets. Smiling she helped her naked slimy Daughter to the kitchen and even helped her sit. Five pound chunks of slightly cooked meat were put in our bowls. You better believe we were drooling bad. That floor was gonna need a mop!

After dinner us Dogs went to the Den while they both went their separate ways. Gift wrapping time it seemed. Well two could play at that game! Okay six! Getting easier for me to communicate with them so I had the Boys watch for either of the humans while I was naughty. Now I am not a computer wizard but I hoped I did not have to be. Turned out to be easy though. Yes like most people he had easy passwords at home. All his card numbers were stored on his computer as well. He owed me five hundred bucks still so I spent it!

Checked things on a hunch however which proved to be right! Tweaked it a bit. Loved my new family. Sent a message to my brother telling him I was fine and happy and loved him! Did not cover my tracks on this computer. On a sudden second hunch I typed in my new name! Found exactly what I suspected I would now. Did not understand it all but got enough of it. Left the file right there on the screen open for Laura. She would understand now! Who and what I was!

Becky came in first and unaware anything bad had been done by any Dog just cuddled with us Dogs. Laura came in and went calmly to the desk like normal. Froze as she sat down her eyes spotting the screen. She looked quickly over at me! Well I looked at the ceiling. Ooh a cobweb! She was intense as she read and looked at both what I had done and found. She was so intense she was like making weird trilling sounds as she was so intent on what I found and all of us were really looking at her. The Boys seemed unsure of this behavior but from Becky's reaction I felt this was normal in her Mom. Well not normal but not unheard of. Becky pushed me in her Mom's direction somehow understanding.

Got the message however. Went to Laura nervously and pushed my head on her lap. She just began to cry as she stroked my head. Looking down at me she said. "Thank you Athena! And you are so very welcome. We will take care of you forever hunny." Might have too now might she not. Interesting information in that file! All the answers of who and what I was! Also the fact that the Professor had been watching ME for a while! Had my whole life on that computer it seemed! Was the perfect victim for his needs so to speak. Knew about my past before I came and had even pushed them to accept me here. Thought I was just lucky. He knew I was most likely willing but also that I had survived when I should not have. He had investigated many applicants to the college. Mallory stuck out quickly.

Becky looked at us very concerned by her Mothers tears. "What's wrong Mom?" Heard the fear in her voice now.

Laura looked at her Daughter with such sadness on her face. Tears flowed. "Athena may become nothing but a regular Dog very soon hunny! No longer able to act or think like a human ever again! Not sure she cares though. Your Father has done something truly amazing! May have actually done the impossible finally! Her behaviors are definitely Canine already that's for certain. The Nanos are doing way more than healing! They are rewriting her brain as well as body into a Dog. It was the way your Father designed it after all! It would heal any Canine injury in time. Even brain damage. These Bots are unbelievable but locked in a certain way. He knew Athena was going to die! Had done lots to keep her alive that long. He used the first Athena's blood for the DNA and some brainwaves he took from her before she passed, probably more, to tell the bots what to do. He knew you would be devastated by her death and was already trying to save you that pain." So I was nodding mostly. Had something to tell them yet however.

Pushed Laura out of the way and opening my document I typed. They read my words as I did. "It is okay. Do not be sad for me! I was never happy as a human. Happy now. Can be just a Dog for the rest of my life if it happens. Think I am done changing though. What I am now is what I will always be." Felt certain of that really. No idea how to explain what was happening in me but I understood.

Laura sounded skeptical about that however as she asked. "Why?"

More typing. "Talked to bots inside me. Told them thank you. That I was good now and they could stop. Think they have. Don't feel them active any more." Happily I typed. "Can have Puppy's now though. I know!" The Professor was searching for a willing victim long before he had the bots ready. He knew what they would do. Well so he thought. Individually the bots were mindless but collectively? Still not super intelligent they let me choose.

Oh I was hugged half to death by both Women and it degenerated quickly into a cuddle fest. We ended up in Laura's bed were we each took a Dog-Cock in the ass! Sang Christmas carols while butt to butt and those huge things throbbed inside us. This was not the Professors bedroom you understand as they had separate rooms, but it to had its own bathroom. They had separate rooms more because they kept different hours most of their marriage. Us Dogs went outside potty. Came back and I saw the seat was up on the toilet in Laura's potty! Went and looking in. Found a treat. Both humans had pooped and peed. For me? Did not flush! The flavors were wonderful. Tasted them both and knew their flavor in my heart. Truly felt loved now. That is a Dog thing! At least I truly hope it was.

CHAPTER 7 CHRISTMAS MORNING AND ELFNAPPING
Tuesday December 25th

Woke to an odd noise downstairs. A sound that seemed mighty darn sneaky to me. Was early but almost time to get up. Did someone forget something? Well two could play that sneaky game now. Slinking off the bed very careful so as too not wake anyone I crept silently down the stairs in the early morning hours. Very early morning hours! Okay a bit past five. There was a way to get around the house and not turn the lights on! Without barking. Becky told me how.

In the Livingroom! A big shadowy figure that was not wearing red was placing some things beneath the tree! With his back to me! Big mistake there! Bet they would never do that again! Never bend over in front of me fake Santa! Creep slowly closer and at the last second! SNOUT LUNGE! In the Butt! Oh he jumped! Was already certain who it was though and He damn well deserved this one! Well I could say thanks to him later. At the moment it was revenge time! Well if he had just told me I could be a Dog and live with him I may not have believed I would be a real Dog but if he wanted to lead me as a naked human Girl around on a leash? Maybe the occasional rolled up newspaper? Might have said yes! Probably would have as only death was ahead of me. The Professor however never made a sound as he jumped which impressed me. Lights came on though. Not too bright. He turned and was suddenly looking at me with something a lot like awe in his eyes. Amazed at what he had done! "Look on my works ye mighty and despair!" Did Alexander? I hear he wept.

He went to one knee shaking with emotion fast and he just began crying. "I'm sorry Mallory! I did not intend this! I…" Well I was shaking my head. Do not lie to me anymore Professor. True? He had intended for me to become all Dog but I wasn't! He saw not what he intended so it was not a lie! Just wanted me a pet for his Daughter! Expected me to look just like the original Athena! Knew she would treat me so nice for the rest of my life! He did not know if it would make a regular Dog live longer for certain so found something with a long life span to become Athena! Was after all supposed to be Becky's Christmas present! Supposed to be the old Athena in every way however! What he created was not a species specific healing bot but a single animal healing bot! The bots needed DNA to copy when repairing. Sure it could be used on humans if you had their DNA before they were injured however! Bots needed programming to the individual and that took time! Very expensive as well!

Some of the Bots were growing different inside me now. Thanks to me as well. Was supposed to be like the original Athena in every way. Think and act like her. All for Becky! He was never able to show his emotions well but he loved his Daughter. The Bots however had asked me what I wanted.

Speaking of time however! Time for me to say thank you. He never moved. Okay, not by himself! Well I mean I pushed him over and was on him licking his face hard! In utter disbelief he stammered. "Y-y-y-you're not mad at me?" Shook my head in his face. Licked his face more. As I began moving down his body he asked nervously. "You like being this?" Did, so I nodded my answer. He talked too much though. Not the time for talking! Spun and plopped my big furry butt on his face. He mumbled stuff into my crotch but I could not understand what as he had a butt in his face. To busy getting his pants off too! How else should I thank him? Actually easy to do with Dog teeth as well. Honest! I was surprised! Was trying to say thank you, you see! One of the presents under the tree snickered around her gag now as she watched. Well the present had looked pretty terrified when I first came in, in the room and she was watching the Professor. Maybe expecting him to rape her? Better not as she belonged to us Dogs! Smiled well when she saw me sneaking up on the Professor though now hadn't she? Understood where she was and why. Time to lick more and put this tongue of mine to the test! Professor penis! Don't lie under me Professor! Oh he was! Protest all you want Mister! Was going to thank you so do not make me bite you! He got really hard fast though as my tongue is amazing. Felt him relax and sigh. Up my tooter! Played with my boobys finally getting into it while I made him groan! Think he got it! THANK YOU!

The present got a very good look at what I was doing and was happily nodding it's approval of my tongue technique the hopeful little Elf Slut. Wrapped my tongue around that hard shaft and slurped. Licked his nuts too. Liked the Dogs Harbles better but I would do this again if he wanted. Maybe I could get him to shave so I did not eat course pubic hairs. Didn't I say before that I would? I think so! Lapped up his tasty Cum when he did. Rather quickly on the squirt I thought. Did little ole me excite him? Naughty old Professor.

Turned around and licked his face clean for him now. Well I had gotten wet and kinda ground my rump on his face. Yes it had some blood in it but not like a period. Ooh he opened his mouth! Scraped the back of his throat. Check his tonsils. Wiggled my tushy on his cock wishing he could already get hard again as I was Hot. Okay in heat! Well Santa had been very nice and I was in heat still after all. Naughty Professor knew I wanted a bone for Christmas now though. Chuckling he said joyfully. "Later Girl. Have to give Daddy some time. You are grateful I know! You're also welcome." Woofed and the tree lights came on now. That tree was utterly spectacular! More so with many new presents under there one of who's face lit up at the beauty. She had not gotten a good look around yet I assumed. Maybe I would get smacked on the rump with a rolled up newspaper later! Was

Christmas after all. A Girl can hope! Is on my Doggy to do list! He looked at the present with the big grin on it's face and said nervously to me. "Swear I had nothing to do with that!" He was not scared however.

Well of course he didn't! I did! Owed Tony and Guido for the quick last minute Christmas kidnapping. Some of the stuff I asked for was here I saw! Hoped they managed everything! Sure it was short notice but they were Mob. They sure did a nice job of wrapping her as well. She was just so pudgy and adorable and if not for the ribbons she was totally naked! Well except for that cute Elf hat! Wanted that on her. Maybe Tony and Guido could come over and help the Professor see how long I can keep standing while dicks were kept in me?! Hey I was in heat! Knew it well by now. Yes that disturbed me in a way but I thought I could encourage the Boys to still fuck me when I was not anymore. If I was interested that is. No idea how I would be yet. Hey it was all new ground to all of us. Would see how things went now wouldn't I?

The Professor looked at the present and asked her very gently. Fatherly even. "Are you okay hunny?" She nodded fast. "Do you want to leave?" She thought for a moment as she looked at me. She knew where she was now. Sort of. Shook her head. No, she was staying! Maybe for a long time! Hoped they got the ransom note to her parents right. Her family was not poor. Well they'd see it when they got back that is so I had time. Note was supposed to read. "We have your Daughter! If you ever want to see her again you will deliver two tons of Dog food to the animal shelter! Athena and the Bark Gang!" It would help those Dogs sure, but a part of me hoped they did not do it as I always wanted an Elf. Must keep my word though. They don't pay she is mine! Had plans for this Elf if not! Professor Murphy looked at me sharply. "Did you have anything to do with this?" Dogs do not lie! Nodded my guilt. Well the tag on her after all read. "For the Boys! From Athena!" She had a tag stuck on a nipple as well. Oh I was planning on using her too. "Get up Athena Girl. I really need to go get a drink. A strong one now!" Ooh! So I did! He looked at the Elf and asked smiling. "Do you have to go potty?" Shrug than nod from the present. He looked at the clock. "Can you hold it for an hour?" She nodded well fast. Kinda hopped she didn't personally. Well why do you think she was on a sheet of plastic? I'd taste it either way though. Professor stood up and his pants just fell about his ankles. Cold snout in the butt crack I am told wakes you up fast. And everyone else in a five mile radius! He yelped good this time. To the Elf again. "I'm sure you will be happy here as the Dogs chew toy but you can leave if you ever want." Did not say exactly that she could stay but close enough I thought.

Okay! Oh I might let her go! Not till after we used the shit out of her at least. And I mean that literally! Oh I hoped so too as I was hungry and wanted to eat it now! It is a Dog thing! Honest! I Swear! Ever wonder what goes through a

Dog's head? Well now you know! Pretty much Sex, Sleep, Food, and Potty with the occasional chase something in there. Yes the line between Potty and Food is a blurry one because quite often one becomes the other! Dogs believe greatly in recycling! Especially food.

Hey I had no problems with that so why should you? The present I saw had tear stains. No idea how long she was awake for I knew she had been scared for a while bound gagged and left under a Christmas tree. Licked her face clean gently in way of an apology then followed the Professor out to the kitchen panting. He had already opened the refrigerator and was just staring in, in awe. "Well that is a lot of Eggnog!" Hey! I was thinking I ordered more then that! Outside still probably. Not much room left in that fridge. Sure hoped however that Dogs could have Eggnog! Like Eggnog!

Was a bad Dog I knew as I looked in there. This was going to be the best Christmas ever. He must have suspected me. Okay I was acting very suspicious! Had a bit of money in my bank account you see. Took out several student loans to go to school and the money for next semester was in there still. Could not go to school any more like this now could I? And no need for school anymore either. So I wiped out the account. Spent the other five hundred from the Professor as well. He could afford it! He had lots of money! Oh I mean lots too! Saw that bank account. And the other two dozen of them. Killing was his business and business was good! Death it seems is highly profitable!

He looked at me with a grin and asked curious. "Thirsty Girl?" Was, so I nodded. He nicely filled my food dish with eggnog and I thought. "Hell yeah! Good Boy." Got a carton out for himself. Drank out of it. Why dirty a glass! With a half smile he looked at me and asked seriously. "Both hams than?" So I just nodded. "Company is coming then?" Nodded more. He knew I was responsible for most of this if not sure how yet. Not mad either and that was the important part. Was not easy or cheap to work this on Christmas eve but people were willing to do things to please Tony! Tony thought it was all hilarious! And as long as the Elf did not press charges completely legal. So the Professor got the big Turkey and both hams out and in the oven. Thankfully it was a really big oven! Had room for pies and stuff still. Had never had a big Christmas before! My first Christmas as a Dog was going to be very memorable or so help me I was biting someone. The Professor looked cute in his pink frilly apron too. Okay it was Laura's but he wore it!

He was really good in the kitchen too I saw! Cutting up potatoes and stuff quickly for our meal. Just enjoying himself as he prepped. Cooking is a science after all! Like Chemistry with complex compounds.

Becky came stumbling in the kitchen not awake yet and her eyes went wide suddenly with awe and joy. "DADDY! You're alive!" Becky squealed so loud and was in her Father's arms in a flash. Bare naked still of course. The Professor never hesitated however and just hugged her back. Got the powerful idea Becky had never learned it is polite to keep your clothes on. Hey I was good with that though. Clothes suck! Never again!

The Professor took offense at something though and demanded loudly his voice incredulous. "Laura? What lies have you been telling her?"

Laura snickered hard from the doorway. Also naked. "Hey, I told her they were not good enough to kill you but she just would not listen." Laura had been stroking Apollo standing there still naked herself but something got her curious. Maybe all the food? Possible I guess. There was lots out here! No cobwebs though. In silence she went and looked in the oven and Apollo snouted her. Then she looked in the fridge and Apollo snouted her bare butt yet again. "Enough food dear? Corner the market on eggnog?" Oops. She suspected him.

He pointed at me quickly the coward and I held my head high! His voice full of desperation saying. "Talk to the new Dog!" He snickered with Becky though.

Laura looked down at me with awe in her eyes. Her voice firm but not angry. "You did this Athena?" Nod. "How?"

The Professor laughed heartily at that. "The food was probably easy to get compared to the presents under the tree. Especially the big one!"

The Girls went quickly now to see what was there. Probably in fear and we all followed. "Oh my God!" Laura exclaimed turning to me. "What have you done?"

Becky snicker snorted happily. "Kidnapped an Elf it seems. Shes so cute under there too!" Sad eyes up at her Mom. "Can we keep her Mom? We really need an Elf!" The Elf was nodding.

The Professor snort snickered. "We should really let the Dogs unwrap her now. She may have to go potty soon. Get her Girl get the present!" Did not need more instruction. We tore the ribbons from her and licked Elf hard. Looking around quick now I pushed a present over to her.

Looking shocked as she sat up the Elf said. "It has my name on it!" Yep! It sure did. Not easy to get this but I was a decent kidnapper and was willing to go the whole nine yards. Had some talented accomplices as well!

"Better open it then now." Laura said so sweetly standing off to the side now snickering herself. The Elf was not yelling or stuff and seemed rather happy so Mom was fine about it. Dogs can smell emotions you know. Knew how sad and Lonely the Elf truly was back in the mall. Dogs are about family and do not believe in anyone being lonely!

The naked Elf tore her present open and her eyes went wide in shock, awe, and joy! Not easy getting a good Dog costume on Christmas eve. The collar and leash were easy though. One mighty shocked Elf said with awe. "I don't believe it? The Tag on the collar even has my name on it too!" She looked at me and smiled. Laura and Becky came over and put it all on her just a smiling as she blushed thanking them and me. Was so very cute naked! Almost a shame to put the costume on her! The Professor went back to the kitchen just a snickering his tushy off. The second owner tag had Laura's name and the address here on it. That got me some questions. Pushed a Present to Becky instead of answering. Got hugged before she even opened it. Looked the same as the one the Elf had opened after all so she knew. Tara was a Doberman Pincher now, Becky would be a Dalmatian! They knew they would both be Dogs for a while! Canine Christmas!

Potty time however. We Dogs herded them two new Dogs to the kitchen snickering and forced those Bitches out the back door on all fours. Had to show them the ropes after all. Costumes were modified you see. Not easy at all! No more crotch! How could they Potty with out a hole back there? Better question? How could they be Fucked like the Bitches we were gonna make them? Was getting some better suits made soon. On the Professor's money! Worked for now though and both Girls went potty successfully in the snow just a giggling. Made them sniff each others and ours. Yeah, I may have eaten some Elf poop. Good Elf Poop! Did not taste like peppermint though. Inside I made them lap up Eggnog like good Dogs! They honestly seemed to be having loads of fun acting like Dogs for now at least as the giggles told the truth. The Boys were being nice and having fun rubbing and hip bumping them. Dog flirting! Wondered if both Girls were thinking the same thing as the Boys were! Oh I knew the Boys wanted it. Had been there after all. Bitches were horny too. Dogs have no problems fucking a Bitch in the kitchen with her parents watching you see.

Also knew what else the Boys were thinking. Three Bitch's now so no more waiting! My only wonder now was who would get who first! The Dog costumes were thick so would not tear easy from a dew claw. Kept the Girls warmer outside too! Well except for that cold breeze up the butt. And those breasts hanging out! They had cute furry snouts that strapped on their heads even. Yes I owed Tony the Squid a lot now. He liked the way I thought however and he got a good laugh out of it so it was good. Sure I had to promise my first born child I mean Puppy but I knew there would be several soon.

Went to the Professor and sat on my haunches waiting like a good Girl should. He finally looked down at me smiling and asked. "Yes Girl, you want something?"

Nodding I spoke. As well as I could. "Ank ooo addy!"

Oh what that caused! He was a multi-tasker and had a laptop on the counter looking. Laura had shown him my story. He knew most of it though and went to a knee and I was in his arms in a shot as he cried sweetly. "You're welcome sweety. God I was so worryed about you after what I did. Drove myself half crazy but I was able to check in and see things and you absolutely shocked me. No idea why the Boys just attacked you like that however." He sounded honest about that. I knew.

Laura interrupted quick with a snicker. "She was starting her period hunny. Beat half to death too dear in case you had not noticed!" He scoffed in shock. "He never notices the little details. That was what activated your Nanos so strongly dear. She was in such a weird head-space and starved for affection and you know how loving the Boys are? May have raped her at first but she felt their love and showed her own back."

He sounded rather embarrassed now. "That explains a lot." He was lying mostly! He knew who I was! Had known for some time. He set me up. Had several plans to get me out here. Did not know about my period however but he knew I was in big trouble. Had been watching me for a while. Nothing he could do about it that would not most likely get me killed so he just watched. The papers I had seen him going over all the time were to finish the Bots. He loved Becky so he planned to make me Athena for her! Knew I was a dead Girl walking and I would be better off as a Dog after all. Thought I would go full Athena though! He knew most but not everything. The best laid plans of Dogs and Men!

Fenrir was sniffing at Tara Dog's butt as she drank. The Professor seeing this smiled and said. "Get her Boy! Get the Bitch!" Had not planed this part but he was flexible and understood much.

Tara Dog's face was in shock before Fenrir mounted her. The look after was cool. My thoughts? Better get used to being called a Bitch Elf. You were going to be one for the foreseeable future! Maybe forever!

Well that started something as well. Apollo was on Becky just a humping away hard and fast and she was just a grinning as he stuffed her full. Maybe getting plowed by big Dog-Cock in front of her own Father made it more exciting for her but she was drooling quick. He may have been excited as well. After all it's not everyday you see your Daughter and an Elf get plowed by brute Dogs. She had the hat on still! Not letting her take it off! Ever! Staple it to her head if I had too! So cute in it you see. The Naughty Professor held me while Cerberus mounted me. He said happily. "Hope you have Puppys Girl!" Oh I knew I would be pregnant soon if I was not already. Nanobots told me this somehow. Was weird but I felt them as a part of me now.

Well the two humans, I thought of the Girls as Dogs while they were in their costumes, went and began prepping things for the meal. Lots of time before guests arrived sure, but there was lots to cook! They did not know much about the guests. Laura and the Professor worked well together I thought! Surprised me a bit. Separate bedrooms would usually indicate a rift of some sort! Then again if they had very different work schedules it may be a practical thing I thought then. By the very nature of their work they had conflicts. Twenty four hour binges without sleep or longer? Was understandable.

A knock sounded on the front door and I checked for more cobwebs trying to look innocent! Laura glared at me and went to answer it and I quickly looked at the clock. They were early! It would still be okay though I thought. Sounds of shocked delight and many happy voices came our way from the front hall. Told you I was a Bad Dog! Four very beautiful Women and two dashing Men and a Sasquatch came happily into the kitchen with Laura. "Guess what dear? We have company for dinner! The new Dog invited them!" She looked at me sternly. Oops! She smiled quickly however. "It's okay Athena. Actually I should say thanks to you for this Girl. Felt kinda bad last night I had not invited them myself. They did us a big favor and that makes them almost family after all!"

Tony spoke up all smiles holding out a hand to the Professor. "Hi Professor Murphy. I'm Tony the Squid." The big boob twins, oh they were huge, Double D cup at least, cute too, snickered at the nick name. Okay they may have snickered for other reasons! Tony may live up to that name still! "This is my associate Guido the Sledge and his lovely wife Marla." She barely came to Guido's waist. 4'2" Maybe? At best! Very cute Dwarf! She could give Guido a blowjob while standing up I thought! Oh you wish! Yeah I wanted to see that too. Well I was a Dog and Dogs are curious creatures! Never enjoyed sex much while human. Can you blame me? Maybe I would as a Dog! So far I had immensely but I was in heat! "This fine upstanding citizen is Icepick Vinney and his Girlfriend Tina." She was adorable in a Girl next door kinda way. Looked sweet and gentle. Icepick just looked extremely dangerous! He was smiling however. A pleasant smile! "These two lovely Ladys are the Parker twins. Lisa and Bambi! No idea which is which." Biggest tits I had seen in a long time if ever. Looked real too! Strippers? Would they give me a private show as a present?

Gorgeous Girls!

Laura introduced us to everyone. Even us Dogs. Called both Tara and Becky Bitches as well. For the time being they were! Made them Dog Girls blush good. Wagged their Tushy's good however. Laura and the Professor were just accepting of their Daughter's Doggyness. She was happy now and they would do or accept anything that made her happy. People had died for her happiness already! Well I actually was a Dog so I was good with it. Nice to be a Dog! They did not seem to mind that either. These new Women looked at me thoroughly but I was cool! More joy so far in one Christmas than all the rest in my life put together and it was not ten o'clock yet! The Boys had come out, of us, and were checking out the guests all friendly like. Tongues out and slobber ready!

Of course the Boys red rockets were still out. Us Bitches had cum running down our legs but our tongues were out all happy too. Marla was looking hard at the rockets and I wondered if she liked them. Then in a squeaky cute adorable voice she said to her Sasquatch. "Gee Guido their almost as big as you!" The reaction at that was to say the very least, mixed. Guido is a freak of nature in many ways it turns out. Nothing bad mind you. Maybe lots good. Still I never knew Sasquatch could blush! Every one could see how big the rockets were and a few looked at Guido! Yeah me too! But he didn't offer to show us. Shame!

Tony explained to the Professor and Laura everything that had been done last night, by me, and claimed I blackmailed him and blamed me for everything. Cowards! My text messages. Kidnapping of an Elf. Picking up supplys! Sneak in the house with everything. When Laura and the Professor found out the security system was turned off on purpose I got a look or two. If they had a newspaper I am sure they would have used it then. Well that computer could control everything. That I had invited Tony and his associates was okay though it seemed. Well it was not directly but the Professor and Laura had killed thousands so these guys were amateurs. They were very friendly with us before. Least I could do for them! Hey they picked up the grocery's and the presents for me after all. Well of course I consider the Elf a present! Wouldn't you? She was wrapped up and under the tree like one after all. What would you call her? Tony looked at my present finally and said very apologetically. "Sorry if we scared you last night Miss but the Dog said you were going to be very happy here and would not if left at home alone." Tara was nodding now. Happy Dog! "And who doesn't like a good kidnapping?!" That got laughs. Even from the Professor and Laura. Um they used to create weapons of mass destruction!

Kinda kidnapped me now didn't you Professor?

They all pitched in to help with the cooking and it felt like a party! Better? Like a family! Yeah yeah yeah! Most of us were murderers sure! Hey murderers are people too! They celebrate Christmas just like you! Usually. Well I liked these murderers a lot. They were my friends now! Yep smelled them all to make sure! Stuck my snout in every butt there! More than once. Even my own. Had an itch! Got Guido again. His wife made me! Yeah I know it was too easy still. Good thing we have high ceilings. Liked the Twins butts! Did not actually smell alike. Had to check several times to be certain butt their was a difference! Honest! My new family! Hoped so! You can actually chose your Family! However it is illegal to shoot your relatives!

Absolutely everyone seemed to be having fun. The Parker Twins were not much help in the kitchen as they barely cooked but Guido's Wife Marla was a pro! Had to be too feed Guido she said. Icepick was practically a master chef! His skills with a knife were very amazing. There are practical uses for most killing talents. They were all getting along nicely it seemed so I felt good.

Tony was a real joker as well it seems and made us all laugh lots. Right in the middle of a great story about a hit, he told several, something beeped harshly. The Professor went to his computer quickly at that and he suddenly looked pissed and said loud with great anger. "More company is here! Uninvited as well and from the looks of those guns not much in the Christmas Spirit!"

Marla smiled so sweetly as she stood up fast to her four foot height and pulled a 44 Magnum long barrel from her purse. Freaking Cannon! She was so tiny? Looked like a darn Bazooka in her hands! Her voice still so sweet she quipped. "I got the back!" Not to be out done Tina pulled a sawed off shotgun from out of her purse. Big purse she carried! Wondered why earlier? Now I knew!

Laura laughed and said as she headed for her gun which lay on the counter. "I like these people dear!" The Men all smiles headed for the front door trying to out macho each other. The Twins seemed quite genuinely disappointed they had no weapons and could not help at all. Becky motioned them over with a wicked smile and whispered in their ears. Naughty Becky Dalmatian! She knew they had the biggest weapons of all!

The Twins and the new Bitches stayed in the front hall watching. The Boys and me, we were going hunting! Pack style! Really I was a very good student and followed their lead at first. Off through the deep snow we went as MY Family took positions in the driveway. My heart was hammering in my chest with the high pressure excitement I felt. It was a real Hunt! My first Hunt! Gonna kill something! Yes my brain was still whole but I had many Canine characteristics, desires, and morals. Why was up for debate but I felt it was a part of the original Athena I now tapped in a way. Something saying that I needed to stop being a victim in my life! The Bots were in the brain connecting neurons that had not been connected before making me not scared anymore. Maybe even smarter in many ways. The bots were not only turning me into Athena to an extent but also looking for ways to improve! May be why I never went all Dog. Perhaps they felt Mallory/Athena was better then either just Mallory or Athena! Both had desirable quality's after all. They were programmed to make me the best Pet possible for Becky! Instead of transforming me they decided to merge us into one. Could be a better Pet this way! Was Athena in many ways and I would like to blame that for the poop eating at least. Could just be I'm gross and disgusting but I was happy! Caught on quickly as my Canine instincts kicked in and soon I was in the lead Hunting Men! We were not quiet at all either. Snarling and slathering like Rabid Animals as we went! Terror in an enemy is quite useful. Fear and stress create errors and mistakes and I wanted them to make as many as possible. Knew these Men not only outnumbered us but were trained to fight and kill so we needed every advantage we could get. Had a taste for blood from Asshole now and wanted more! Controlled it easy before but now I let it out! Growling and snarling we came on the first two Men from different directions like a bat out of hell and they never got a shot off before we were on them killing! Lots of screams as we rended Flesh gleefully! Cerberus hit the one so hard he drove his Prey back into a tree. Ever been out in the woods and seen those dead branch stumps sticking out of Pine Tree's? Through the upper chest, lower left shoulder and blood spurted. No idea if they were dead yet when we ran off but they were absolutely no threat now. Be dead soon enough!

Racing through the snow we saw two more and went for them hard. Had all their attention you see and they were shooting at us. Oh our noses were amazing and I could talk with the boys to let them know now what was coming. Smelled a third Man. Knew that smell. Vinney earned the name Icepick for good reason. He stepped up behind them like a Ghost without a sound and shoved an Icepick into a skull through the ear silently as we got the other. They panicked and died. Okay maybe they died then panicked! Who cared! Just dead! We could hear that cannon of a 44 thunder and the roar of a shotgun from out back as those Ladys let loose. Knew Men died back there.

We could hear Tony suddenly screaming, all dramatically like in a movie, from the driveway. "Come out and die you bastards! Ruin our Christmas dinner will you!" His twin Colt 45 hand guns roared. Saw a pattern there. He might be crazy but I still liked him! They had him pinned down behind a vehicle, no idea who's, rather quickly though as several were coming up the driveway. Knew he was in trouble and Vinney jerked his head that way and we Dogs went to help looping behind the Men.

Got there just in time to see the Twins come running from the house screaming hysterically. "HELP! Save us!" Bare ass naked! Oh that is an amazing sight! Those breasts were real! Silicone does not bounce like that! Best distraction ever! Tony now laughing stood up from behind his car quick and blasted away at gawking Men like he was born to do it! Impressive! Not as much as those tits but the Grand Canyon would have been jealous! Holy Cleavage Dogman! Tony took out six assholes before they realized they had been had. Apollo and Fenrir were in them in a flash from behind and Laura shot a few strays running for cover having come to the front door now. Oh Cerberus and me? We tackled the Twins. You would not ask why if you could see them! Oh my lord! How I wished I had a penis then! Doggy strap-on? They screamed louder then the dying ones now. Naked in the snow bank so it was to be expected I guess! They were very happy after we ate them though. Cold but happy. Did not want them shot in the crossfire so it was a protective move! Honest! Becky and Tara came out once the shooting stopped and lapped some twin pussy too! All us Dogs had a taste while humans looked for strays. Well if we hadn't tackled the Twins they may have gotten shot! For their own safety after all! And as long as we had them down there? Well you understand I hope! Ate them to warm them up.

Okay I was thinking is everyone out here a pervert? The Doberman Elf was loving licking Bimbo-Pussy! They admitted they were Bimbos! Proud of it too! Well I sure liked Bimbos! Twins never said No, Don't, or Stop!

Laura finally whistled sharply and we stopped. Damn it! They came and helped the Twins up out of the snow and most snickered at the butt prints. As they all walked to the house smiling Tony snickered at the Twins. "Better run girls. Pack HUNT!" Herded those two into the den and well. They were little help in the kitchen really so we kept them busy. Maybe they would have Puppys! Might be part Dog after all! Could drool real well! Happy Bimbos!

Laura yelled food would not be ready for an hour. Odd that as I was actually eating at that moment. What food was she talking about? This food was darn tasty! Not filling but very tasty! Well Becky and Tara were both getting pounded along with a Twin. Did not want the other to feel left out you see so I ate her. Was always a good hostess. Felt a hand on my butt after a while. Lifted my head out of Bimbo-Pussy and looked back at Tony who smiled down at me. "Came to see if anyone needed any help." Funny he should say that cause I could use something to help! Cocked my tail to the side. What a grin now! "Good thing I came then isn't it" He better not have come yet! "Okay I see my help is needed in here and my dates are currently occupied." For emphasis he pushed a finger in me. His other hand was undoing his pants. Finger out I felt hard Italian Gangster-Cock rubbing me. Did I excite him? Oh Tony! He was mighty big and he knew what to do with it. Humped me just like a Dog too! How sweet of him. All hands as well. He owned that name well I found out! Liked my eight furry tits it seemed! Knew why they call him the Squid! Nice to get all my tits fondled however! Did owe him still now didn't I? Sure we were having sex and yes people may be dying outside still. They better just get on with it and cut down on the surplus population of Assholes, was all I could think. Sorry Chuck! No I didn't care! Sure my morals were very different now. They came here with big guns to kill us all. On Christmas! They killed Kenny the Bastards! Well I did not think Kenny the tree would live. So they all died on Christmas just like Jesus! Oops! Wait! He was born April first! Honest!

We got caught though. First I noticed, hard to hear over this twins squeals, was when Vinney said. "You know if the boss had not caught Tony fucking Dorthy we would not be stuck out here." They must have looked at him as he explained. "Dorthy was the bosses Wife's prize show Poodle! Gorgeous Bitch. Loved Tony! He loved her! To much perhaps?" Tony must have given him a look. "It's okay Tony! Starting to like here boss. Nice people we found here. Best Christmas I ever had!" Much agreement there. Well it was for me also. The Professor and Laura dealt in death their whole lives. In part responsible for hundreds of thousands of deaths really. They told some storys as well! The Gangsters were jealous.

The Christmas meal was amazing and plentiful. They had done great stuff in the kitchen! Us Dogs got lots! The company was truly delightful! The Elf said sweetly. "And God bless us! Everyone!" Sorry again Chuck. Nothing like killing together to bring people closer! The only disappointment I had was they made us let the Twins get dressed! Might have Made the twins get dressed as well since the Twins may have been disappointed too!

Couldn't wait for New Years!

We wish you a Merry Canine Christmas!